THE USBORNE PICTURE ATLAS

Revised Edition

Edited by Jenny Tyler and Lisa Watts
Designed by John Strange
Map adviser: Yolande O'Donoghue,
Map Library, British Library Reference Division.

First published in 1976 by Usborne Publishing Ltd,
20 Garrick Street, London WC2E 9BJ, England.

Printed in Belgium

Contents

The World

AMERICA 1

ATLANTIC OCEAN

EUROPE 1

Equator

AMERICA 2

PACIFIC OCEAN

How the world is divided up

This is a map of the world. The different colours show how we have divided it up for the maps in this book.

What the maps show

Each map shows the countries, with their capital cities and flags, the largest towns, longest rivers, biggest lakes and highest mountains.

We have found out the four things that each area makes or grows the most of and put picture symbols in the centres of production of each one.

Pictures on and around the maps show the people and their jobs, customs, festivals, sports and crafts, famous buildings, rare wild animals and other important and interesting features of each area.

How to use the scales

Every map has a scale which shows you what 100 km looks like on the page.

To find out how far it is from one place to another, see how many 100 km scale lengths fit between them on the map.

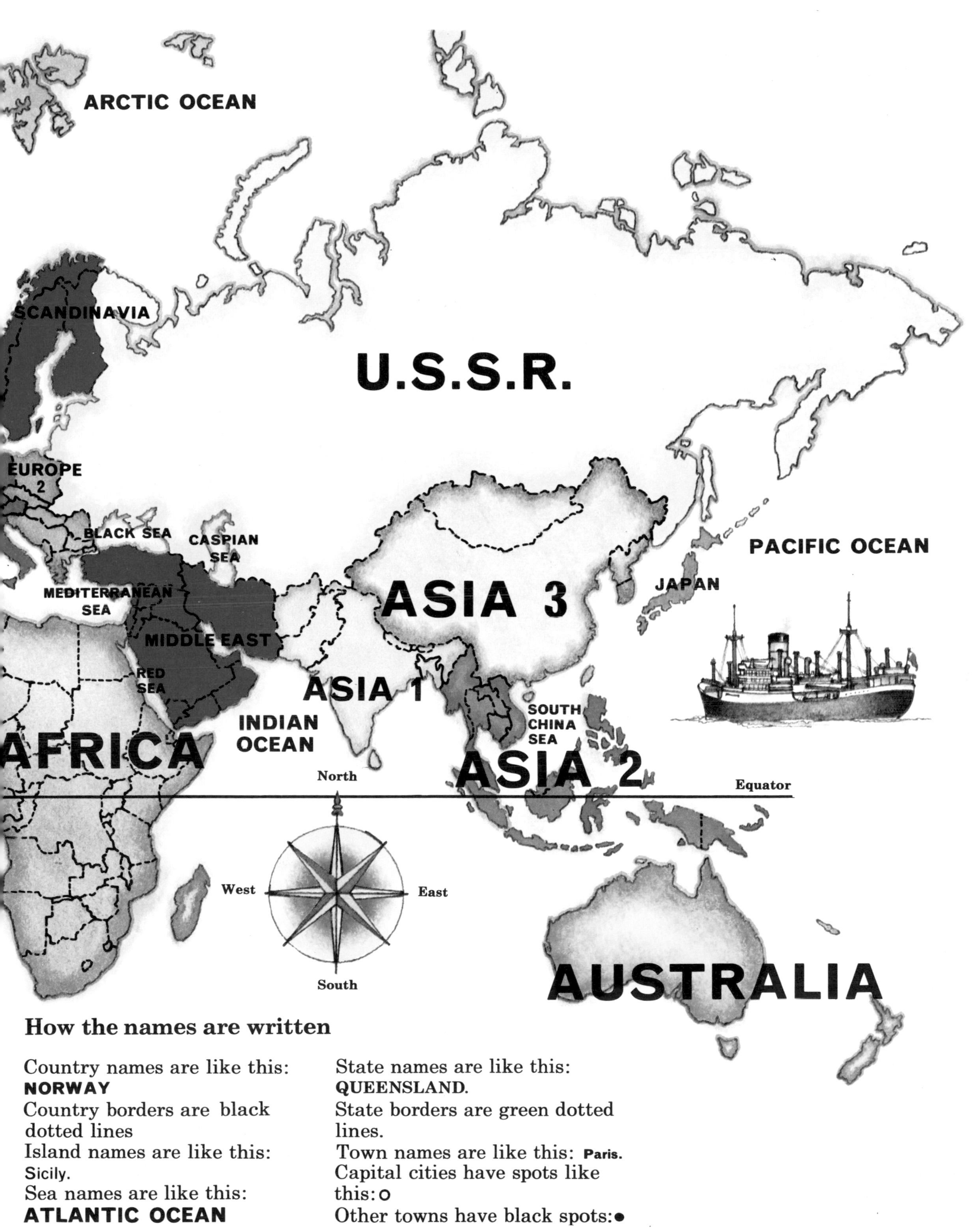
ARCTIC OCEAN
SCANDINAVIA
U.S.S.R.
EUROPE 2
BLACK SEA
CASPIAN SEA
MEDITERRANEAN SEA
MIDDLE EAST
RED SEA
ASIA 3
PACIFIC OCEAN
JAPAN
ASIA 1
INDIAN OCEAN
SOUTH CHINA SEA
AFRICA
ASIA 2
North
Equator
West
East
South
AUSTRALIA

How the names are written

Country names are like this: **NORWAY**
Country borders are black dotted lines
Island names are like this: Sicily.
Sea names are like this: **ATLANTIC OCEAN**

State names are like this: **QUEENSLAND.**
State borders are green dotted lines.
Town names are like this: **Paris.**
Capital cities have spots like this: o
Other towns have black spots: ●

America 1

Canada, the United States of America (U.S.A. for short) and Mexico are the main countries in North America. The U.S.A. is made up of 50 states. Alaska is one of these although it is not joined on to the rest.

The land in the north is iced over and polar bears live there. Thick forest covers the Rocky Mountains and parts of Canada. Further south, there are flat plains where wheat and maize are grown. Much of east U.S.A. is covered with factories and towns.

There are about 340 million people in North America. North American Indians have always lived there. European explorers first found the land nearly 500 years ago, and since then many Europeans have lived there too.

In Canada some people speak English and others French. In Mexico, people speak Spanish.

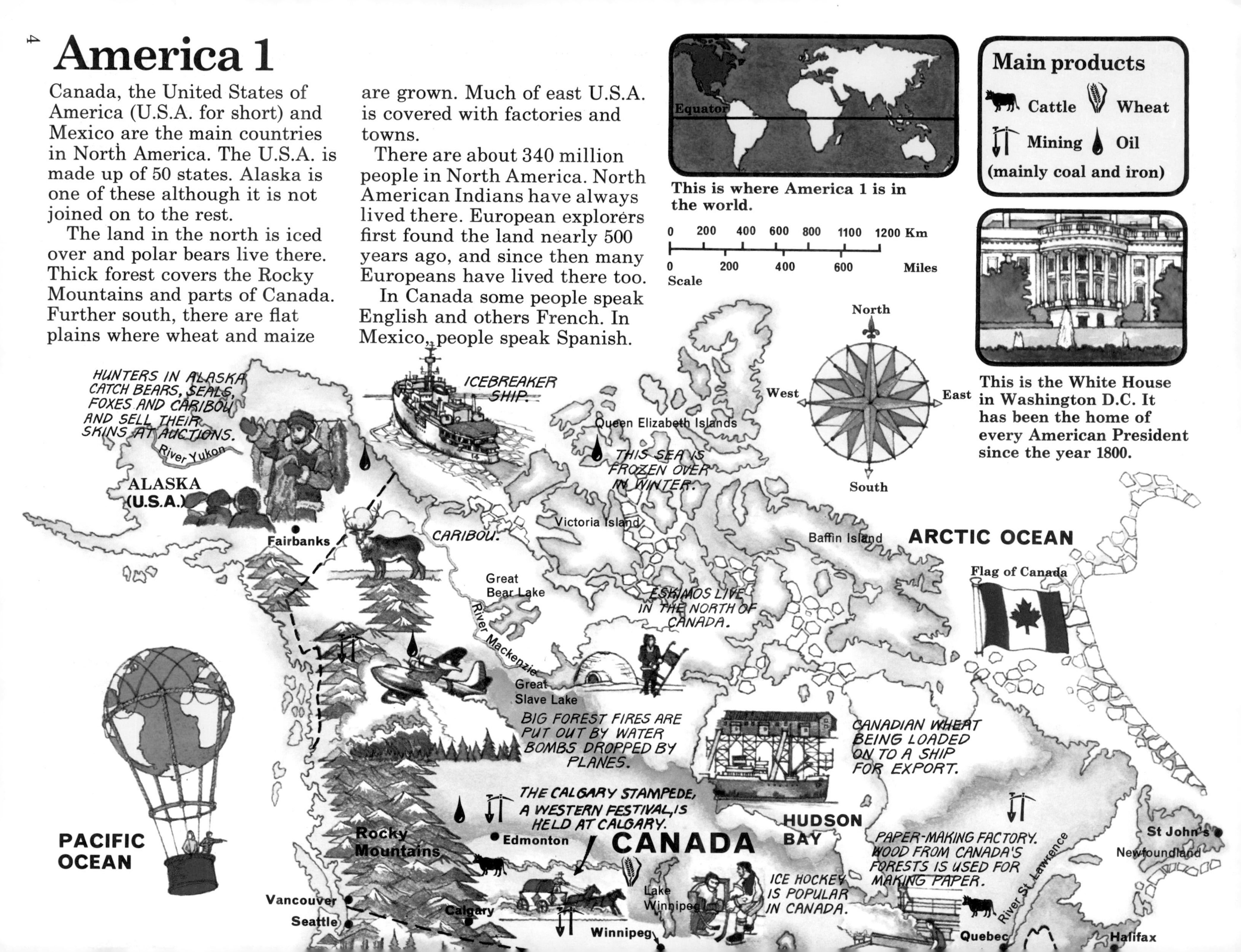
Equator
This is where America 1 is in the world.
0 200 400 600 800 1100 1200 Km
0 200 400 600 Miles
Scale
Main products
Cattle
Wheat
Mining
Oil
(mainly coal and iron)
North
West
East
South
HUNTERS IN ALASKA CATCH BEARS, SEALS, FOXES AND CARIBOU AND SELL THEIR SKINS AT AUCTIONS.
River Yukon
ALASKA (U.S.A.)
Fairbanks
ICEBREAKER SHIP.
Queen Elizabeth Islands
THIS SEA IS FROZEN OVER IN WINTER.
Victoria Island
CARIBOU.
Baffin Island
ARCTIC OCEAN
Flag of Canada
Great Bear Lake
River Mackenzie
ESKIMOS LIVE IN THE NORTH OF CANADA.
Great Slave Lake
BIG FOREST FIRES ARE PUT OUT BY WATER BOMBS DROPPED BY PLANES.
CANADIAN WHEAT BEING LOADED ON TO A SHIP FOR EXPORT.
THE CALGARY STAMPEDE, A WESTERN FESTIVAL, IS HELD AT CALGARY.
PACIFIC OCEAN
Rocky Mountains
Edmonton
CANADA
HUDSON BAY
PAPER-MAKING FACTORY. WOOD FROM CANADA'S FORESTS IS USED FOR MAKING PAPER.
St John's
Newfoundland
River St Lawrence
Lake Winnipeg
ICE HOCKEY IS POPULAR IN CANADA.
Vancouver
Seattle
Calgary
Winnipeg
Quebec
Halifax

This is the White House in Washington D.C. It has been the home of every American President since the year 1800.

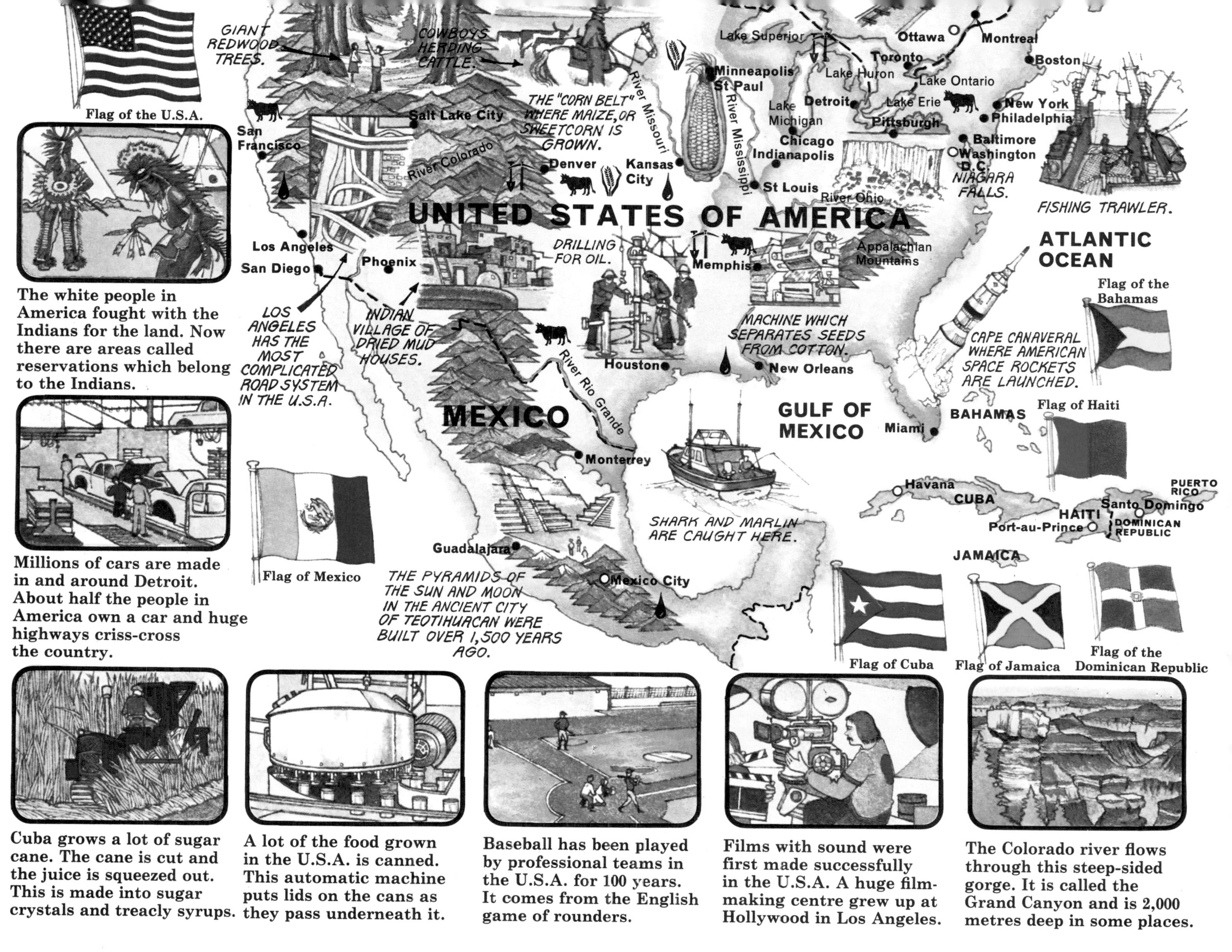
Flag of the U.S.A.
GIANT REDWOOD TREES.
COWBOYS HERDING CATTLE.
THE "CORN BELT" WHERE MAIZE, OR SWEETCORN IS GROWN.
San Francisco
Salt Lake City
River Colorado
Denver
Kansas City
River Missouri
Minneapolis St Paul
River Mississippi
Lake Superior
Lake Michigan
Lake Huron
Ottawa
Montreal
Toronto
Lake Ontario
Lake Erie
Boston
New York
Philadelphia
Detroit
Pittsburgh
Chicago
Indianapolis
Baltimore
Washington D.C.
NIAGARA FALLS.
St Louis
River Ohio
FISHING TRAWLER.
UNITED STATES OF AMERICA
ATLANTIC OCEAN
Los Angeles
San Diego
Phoenix
DRILLING FOR OIL.
Memphis
Appalachian Mountains
LOS ANGELES HAS THE MOST COMPLICATED ROAD SYSTEM IN THE U.S.A.
INDIAN VILLAGE OF DRIED MUD HOUSES.
MACHINE WHICH SEPARATES SEEDS FROM COTTON.
CAPE CANAVERAL WHERE AMERICAN SPACE ROCKETS ARE LAUNCHED.
Flag of the Bahamas
Houston
New Orleans
River Rio Grande
MEXICO
GULF OF MEXICO
Miami
BAHAMAS
Flag of Haiti
Monterrey
Havana
CUBA
PUERTO RICO
Santo Domingo
HAITI
Port-au-Prince
DOMINICAN REPUBLIC
SHARK AND MARLIN ARE CAUGHT HERE.
Guadalajara
JAMAICA
Flag of Mexico
Mexico City
THE PYRAMIDS OF THE SUN AND MOON IN THE ANCIENT CITY OF TEOTIHUACAN WERE BUILT OVER 1,500 YEARS AGO.
Flag of Cuba
Flag of Jamaica
Flag of the Dominican Republic

The white people in America fought with the Indians for the land. Now there are areas called reservations which belong to the Indians.

Millions of cars are made in and around Detroit. About half the people in America own a car and huge highways criss-cross the country.

Cuba grows a lot of sugar cane. The cane is cut and the juice is squeezed out. This is made into sugar crystals and treacly syrups.

A lot of the food grown in the U.S.A. is canned. This automatic machine puts lids on the cans as they pass underneath it.

Baseball has been played by professional teams in the U.S.A. for 100 years. It comes from the English game of rounders.

Films with sound were first made successfully in the U.S.A. A huge film-making centre grew up at Hollywood in Los Angeles.

The Colorado river flows through this steep-sided gorge. It is called the Grand Canyon and is 2,000 metres deep in some places.

America 2

This is South America. It begins above the equator and stretches down almost to Antarctica. It is very cold in the south, especially in winter. In the north, there is hot, steamy rain forest, parts of which are still unexplored.

Until about 400 years ago, the only people living here were South American Indians. Then, Spanish and Portuguese explorers found the land. Many European people came and settled bringing their languages and customs with them. Now there are about 289 million people living in South America.

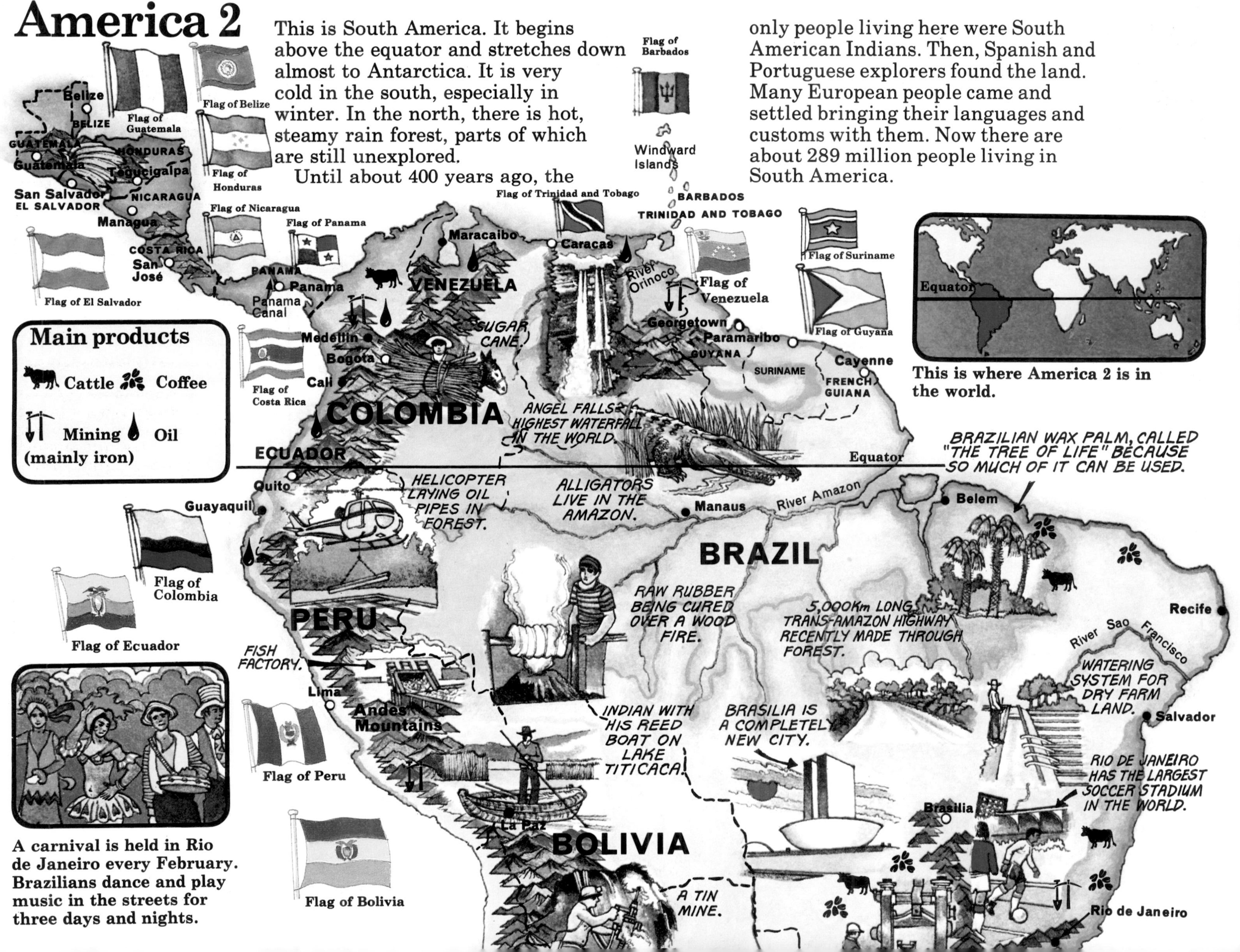
Belize
BELIZE
GUATEMALA
Guatemala
HONDURAS
Tegucigalpa
San Salvador
EL SALVADOR
NICARAGUA
Managua
COSTA RICA
San José
PANAMA
Panama
Panama Canal
Flag of Guatemala
Flag of Belize
Flag of Honduras
Flag of El Salvador
Flag of Nicaragua
Flag of Panama
Flag of Costa Rica
Flag of Barbados
Windward Islands
BARBADOS
TRINIDAD AND TOBAGO
Flag of Trinidad and Tobago
Flag of Venezuela
Flag of Suriname
Flag of Guyana
Main products
Cattle
Coffee
Mining (mainly iron)
Oil
Maracaibo
Caracas
VENEZUELA
River Orinoco
Georgetown
Paramaribo
GUYANA
SURINAME
Cayenne
FRENCH GUIANA
Medellin
Bogota
Cali
SUGAR CANE.
COLOMBIA
ANGEL FALLS HIGHEST WATERFALL IN THE WORLD.
ECUADOR
Equator
Quito
Guayaquil
HELICOPTER LAYING OIL PIPES IN FOREST.
ALLIGATORS LIVE IN THE AMAZON.
Manaus
River Amazon
Belem
BRAZILIAN WAX PALM, CALLED "THE TREE OF LIFE" BECAUSE SO MUCH OF IT CAN BE USED.
BRAZIL
Flag of Colombia
Flag of Ecuador
PERU
RAW RUBBER BEING CURED OVER A WOOD FIRE.
5,000Km LONG TRANS-AMAZON HIGHWAY RECENTLY MADE THROUGH FOREST.
Recife
River Sao Francisco
FISH FACTORY.
Lima
Andes Mountains
INDIAN WITH HIS REED BOAT ON LAKE TITICACA.
BRASILIA IS A COMPLETELY NEW CITY.
WATERING SYSTEM FOR DRY FARM LAND.
Salvador
Flag of Peru
RIO DE JANEIRO HAS THE LARGEST SOCCER STADIUM IN THE WORLD.
Brasilia
La Paz
BOLIVIA
Flag of Bolivia
A TIN MINE.
Rio de Janeiro
Equator

This is where America 2 is in the world.

A carnival is held in Rio de Janeiro every February. Brazilians dance and play music in the streets for three days and nights.

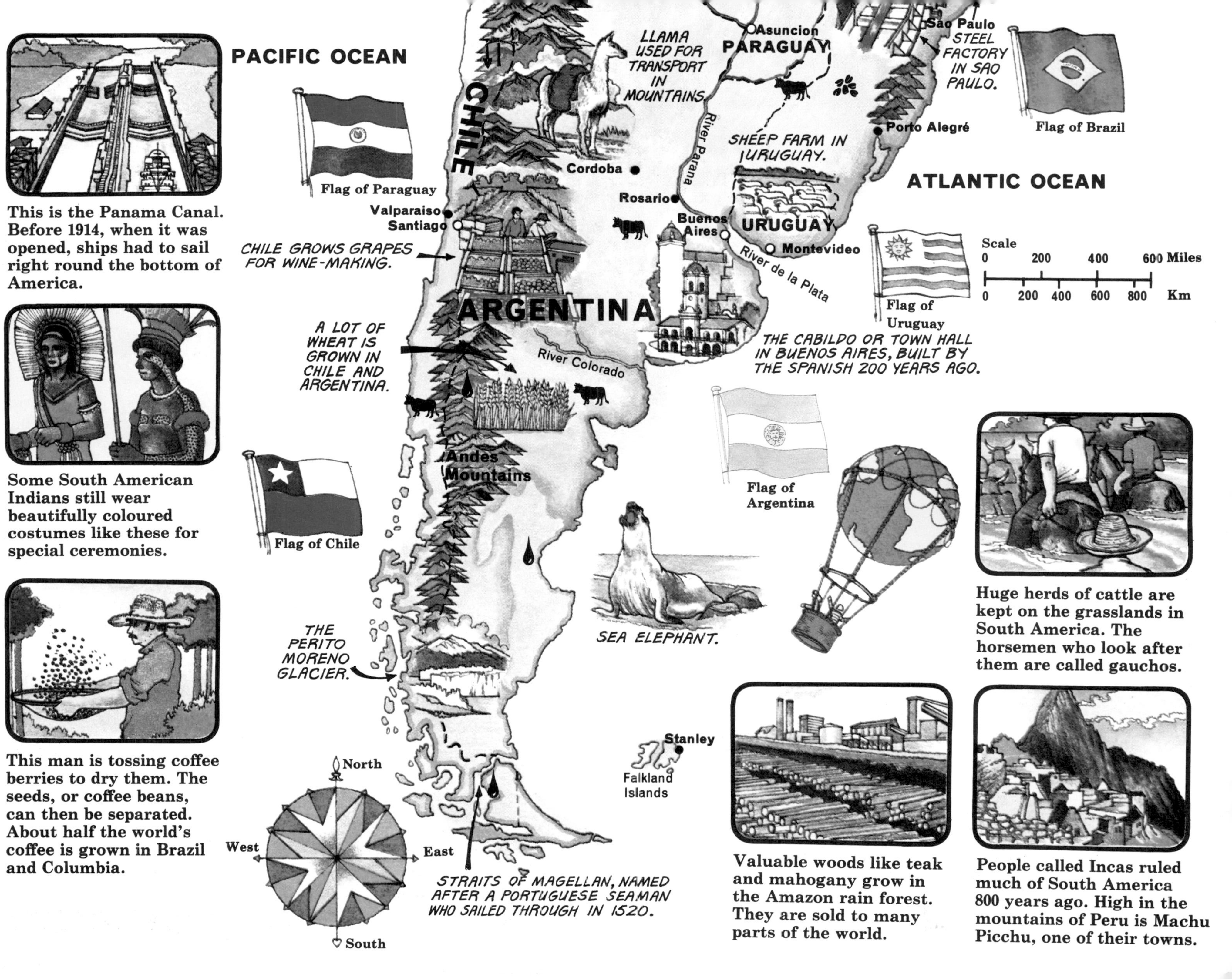
PACIFIC OCEAN
ATLANTIC OCEAN
CHILE
ARGENTINA
PARAGUAY
URUGUAY
Asuncion
Sao Paulo
STEEL FACTORY IN SAO PAULO.
Porto Alegré
Flag of Brazil
LLAMA USED FOR TRANSPORT IN MOUNTAINS
River Parana
SHEEP FARM IN URUGUAY.
Cordoba
Rosario
Buenos Aires
Montevideo
River de la Plata
Flag of Paraguay
Valparaiso
Santiago
CHILE GROWS GRAPES FOR WINE-MAKING.
Flag of Uruguay
Scale
0 200 400 600 Miles
0 200 400 600 800 Km
A LOT OF WHEAT IS GROWN IN CHILE AND ARGENTINA.
River Colorado
THE CABILDO OR TOWN HALL IN BUENOS AIRES, BUILT BY THE SPANISH 200 YEARS AGO.
Flag of Argentina
Andes Mountains
Flag of Chile
SEA ELEPHANT.
THE PERITO MORENO GLACIER.
Stanley
Falkland Islands
North
West
East
South
STRAITS OF MAGELLAN, NAMED AFTER A PORTUGUESE SEAMAN WHO SAILED THROUGH IN 1520.

This is the Panama Canal. Before 1914, when it was opened, ships had to sail right round the bottom of America.

Some South American Indians still wear beautifully coloured costumes like these for special ceremonies.

This man is tossing coffee berries to dry them. The seeds, or coffee beans, can then be separated. About half the world's coffee is grown in Brazil and Columbia.

Huge herds of cattle are kept on the grasslands in South America. The horsemen who look after them are called gauchos.

Valuable woods like teak and mahogany grow in the Amazon rain forest. They are sold to many parts of the world.

People called Incas ruled much of South America 800 years ago. High in the mountains of Peru is Machu Picchu, one of their towns.

Europe 1

This part of Europe is the home of about 338 million people. Germany has the most people, but Belgium and the Netherlands are the most crowded because they are smaller.

In the north it is rainy all the year round and the weather is seldom very hot or very cold. Spain and Italy are called Mediterranean countries because they are on the Mediterranean Sea. Here, the weather is very hot and dry in summer and rainy in winter. Oranges and lemons, olives and cork trees are grown on the hot, dry hills.

The highest mountain in Europe is Mont Blanc in the Alps. High mountains in the Alps and the Pyrenees are covered with snow.

The languages of the countries in the north come mainly from old German. The languages of the other countries come from Latin, which was spoken in Italy 2,000 years ago.

17

In midwinter, cars race through Europe on the Monte Carlo Rally. The finishing line is in Monte Carlo, the capital city of Monaco.

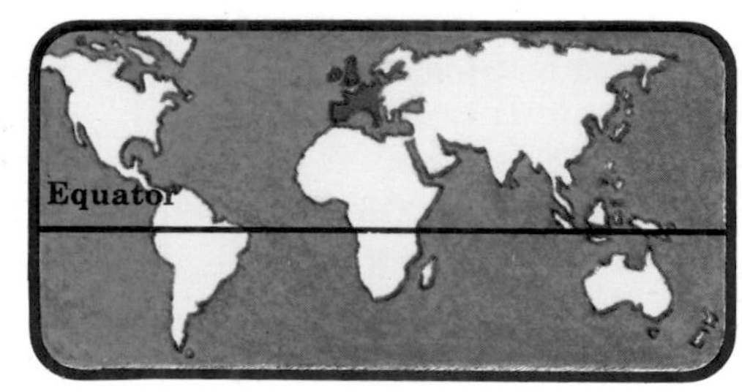
Equator

This is where Europe 1 is in the world.

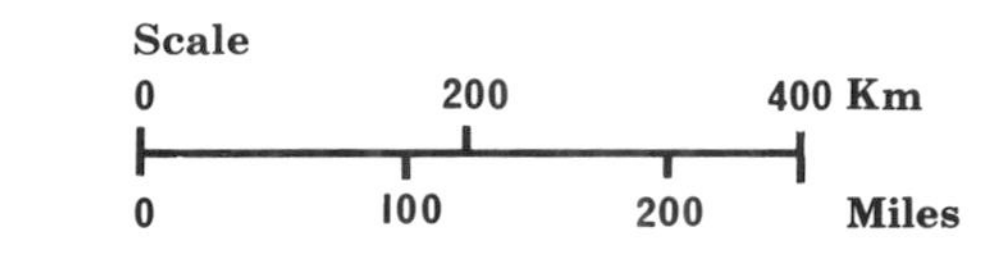
Scale
0
200
400 Km
0
100
200
Miles

Main products

Wheat · Cattle · Wine · Machinery

The river Rhine flows all the way from Switzerland to the Netherlands and then into the sea. River barges carry goods from factories to the ports.

Wine is made from grape juice. Good wine is kept for several years to improve it. Most wine is made in Italy, France and West Germany.

This is a modern milking parlour. Here, the cows are milked by machines and fed at the same time.

Flag of the British Isles

Shetland Islands

Orkney Islands

Hebrides

OIL PLATFORM IN THE NORTH SEA.

SCOTLAND

Aberdeen

GOLDEN EAGLE.

Glasgow

Edinburgh

REPUBLIC OF IRELAND

NORTHERN IRELAND

Belfast

BRITISH ISLES

IRISH LINEN BEING WOVEN.

Dublin

NORTH SEA

Liverpool

Manchester

ENGLAND

WALES

Birmingham

Cardiff

CANTERBURY CATHEDRAL.

London

Southampton

ATLANTIC OCEAN

Flag of the Republic of Ireland

ENGLISH CHANNEL

Flag of Belgium

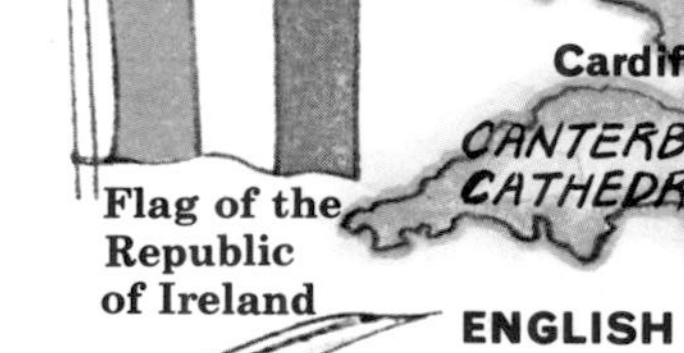

CONCORDE, BUILT BY THE FRENCH AND BRITISH, CAN FLY FASTER THAN SOUND.

Flag of West Germany

Flag of East Germany

Flag of the Netherlands

DUTCH BULBS ARE VERY FAMOUS.

River Elbe

Hamburg

Amsterdam

WEST GERMANY

Rotterdam

NETHERLANDS

Brussels

BELGIUM

Bonn

Cologne

Frankfurt

EAST GERMANY

Berlin

Leipzig

Dresden

THE BERLIN WALL DIVIDES EAST AND WEST BERLIN.

Flag of Luxembourg

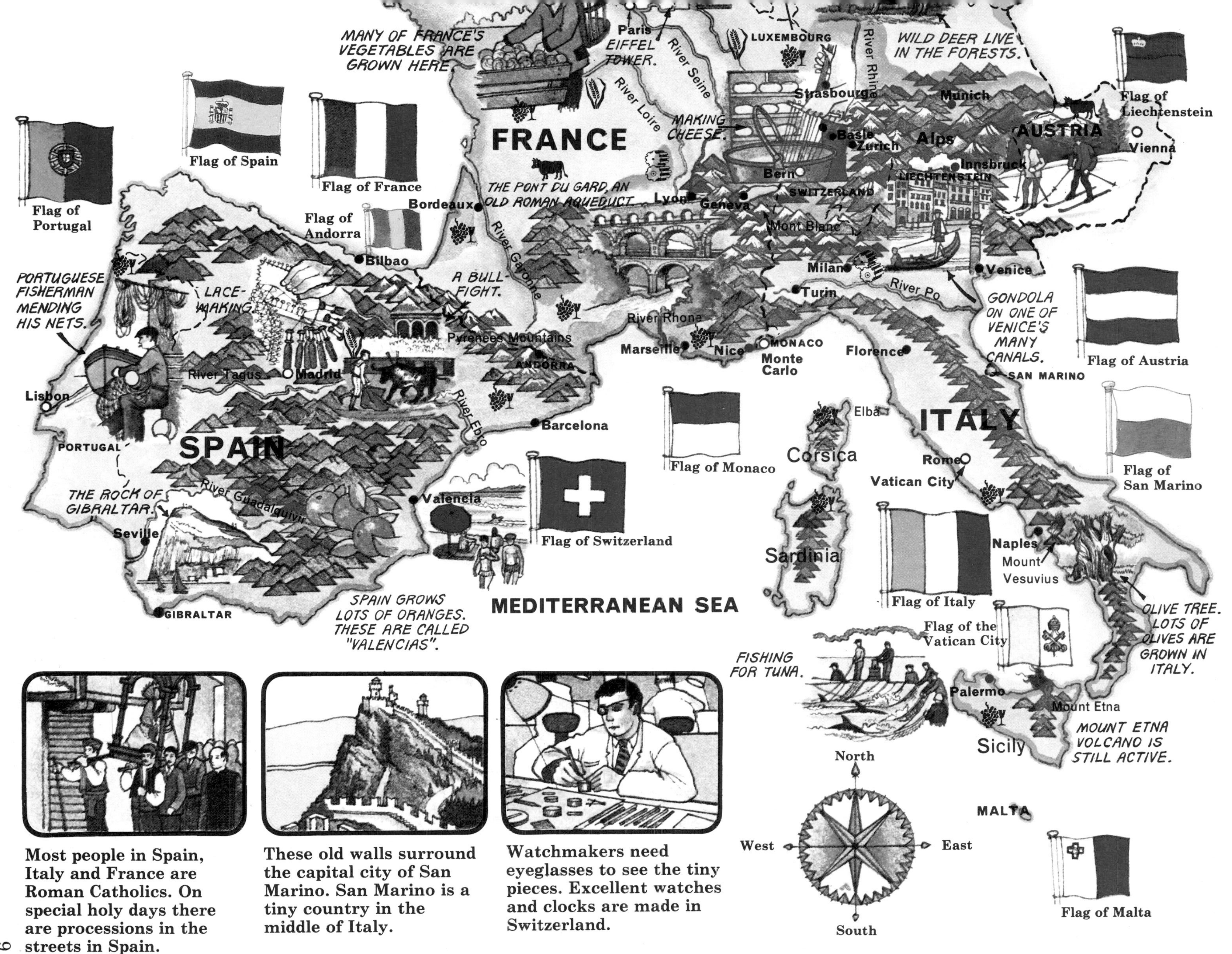
MANY OF FRANCE'S VEGETABLES ARE GROWN HERE
Paris
EIFFEL TOWER.
River Seine
River Loire
LUXEMBOURG
River Rhine
WILD DEER LIVE IN THE FORESTS.
Flag of Liechtenstein
Flag of Spain
Flag of France
Flag of Portugal
FRANCE
MAKING CHEESE.
Strasbourg
Munich
Basle
Zurich
Alps
AUSTRIA
Vienna
Innsbruck
LIECHTENSTEIN
Bern
SWITZERLAND
Lyon
Geneva
THE PONT DU GARD, AN OLD ROMAN AQUEDUCT
Bordeaux
River Garonne
Flag of Andorra
Mont Blanc
Bilbao
A BULL-FIGHT.
Milan
Venice
Turin
River Po
PORTUGUESE FISHERMAN MENDING HIS NETS.
LACE-MAKING
River Rhone
GONDOLA ON ONE OF VENICE'S MANY CANALS.
Flag of Austria
Pyrenees Mountains
Marseille
Nice
MONACO
Monte Carlo
Florence
River Tagus
Madrid
ANDORRA
SAN MARINO
Lisbon
River Ebro
Barcelona
Flag of Monaco
Elba
ITALY
PORTUGAL
SPAIN
Corsica
Rome
Vatican City
Flag of San Marino
THE ROCK OF GIBRALTAR.
River Guadalquivir
Valencia
Flag of Switzerland
Seville
Sardinia
Flag of Italy
Naples
Mount Vesuvius
GIBRALTAR
SPAIN GROWS LOTS OF ORANGES. THESE ARE CALLED "VALENCIAS".
MEDITERRANEAN SEA
Flag of the Vatican City
OLIVE TREE. LOTS OF OLIVES ARE GROWN IN ITALY.
FISHING FOR TUNA.
Palermo
Mount Etna
Sicily
MOUNT ETNA VOLCANO IS STILL ACTIVE.
North
MALTA
West
East
South
Flag of Malta

Most people in Spain, Italy and France are Roman Catholics. On special holy days there are processions in the streets in Spain.

These old walls surround the capital city of San Marino. San Marino is a tiny country in the middle of Italy.

Watchmakers need eyeglasses to see the tiny pieces. Excellent watches and clocks are made in Switzerland.

Europe 2

This is the eastern part of Europe. It stretches from the Baltic Sea in the north to the Mediterranean Sea in the south.

Turkey and Greece are Mediterranean countries. They have hot, dry weather in the summer and some rain in the winter. Olive trees and grape vines grow on their dry, stony hills. Part of Turkey is in Asia and is shown on the Middle East map.

The other countries in eastern Europe also have hot, dry summers, but they are bitterly cold in the winter. The sea round Poland sometimes freezes over.

Much of the land is covered with forest where wild bears and wolves still live. In Hungary and Romania there are large areas of flat grassland through which the River Danube flows on its way to the Black Sea.

There are about 131 million people in this part of Europe.

Equator

This is where Europe 2 is in the world.

Scale: 0 100 200 300 400 Km; 0 100 200 Miles

Main products

Wheat, Sugar beet, Mining (mainly coal), Wine

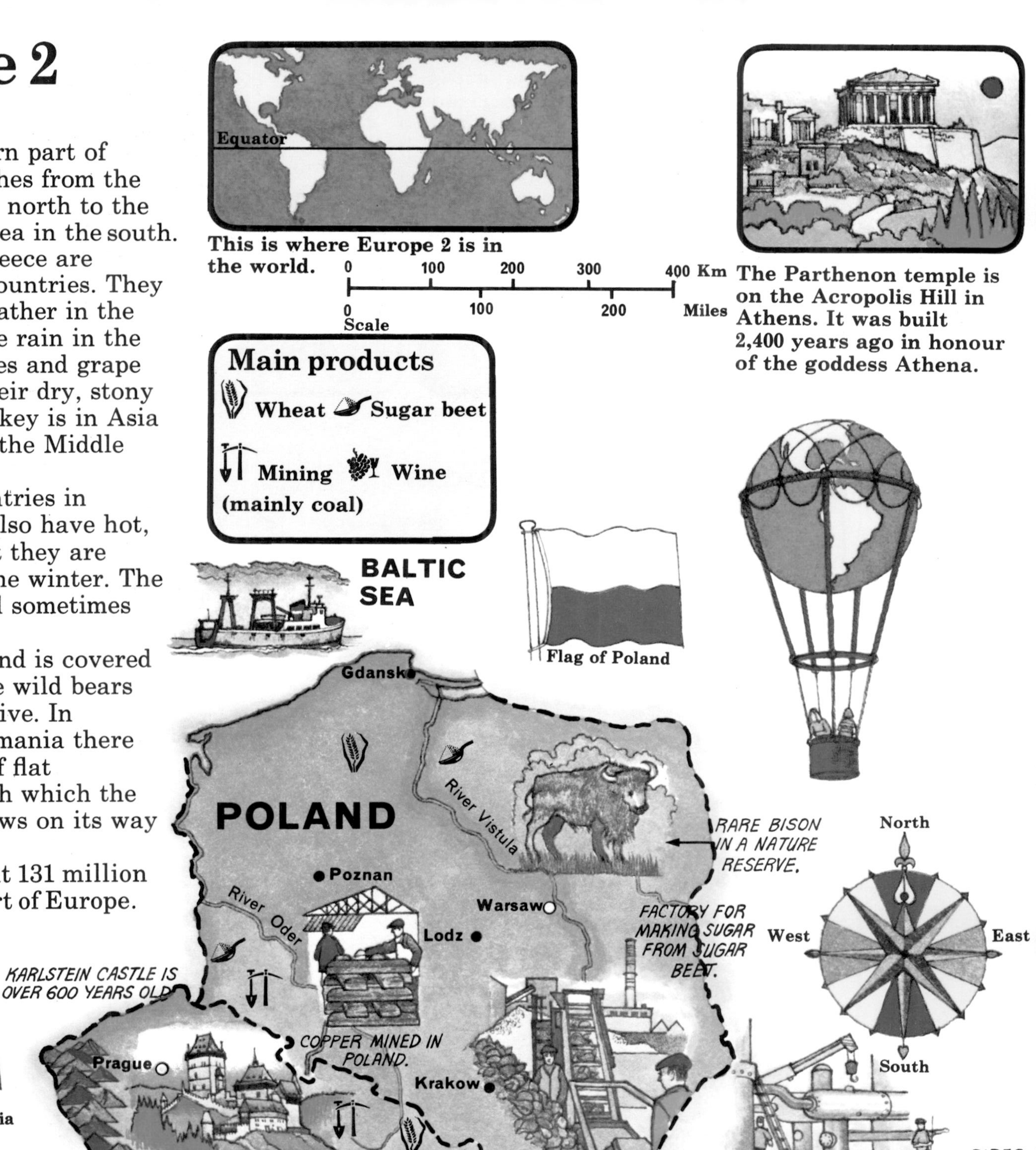

BALTIC SEA
Flag of Poland
Gdansk
POLAND
River Vistula
RARE BISON IN A NATURE RESERVE.
Poznan
River Oder
Warsaw
Lodz
FACTORY FOR MAKING SUGAR FROM SUGAR BEET.
KARLSTEIN CASTLE IS OVER 600 YEARS OLD
COPPER MINED IN POLAND.
Prague
Krakow
Brno
CZECHOSLOVAKIA
Bratislava
Flag of Czechoslovakia
North
West
East
South
PIPES CARRY GAS AND OIL TO CZECHOSLOVAKIA FROM THE U.S.S.R.

The Parthenon temple is on the Acropolis Hill in Athens. It was built 2,400 years ago in honour of the goddess Athena.

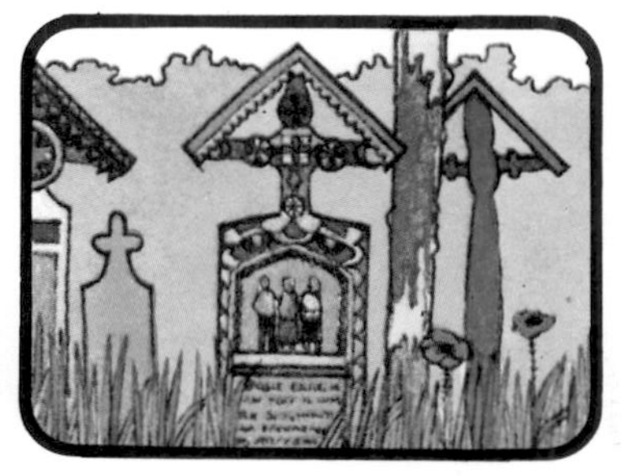

This is the "Merry Cemetery" in Sapinta, Romania. Here it is an old custom to carve the graves and paint them.

The water from some springs in Romania is good for people's health. People have visited them since ancient times.

Tankers and fishing trawlers are made in Polish shipyards. This trawler makes a huge splash as it is launched sideways into the water.

Flag of Hungary
MEDICINES ARE MADE IN HUNGARY.
Budapest
HUNGARY
ROMANIAN SHEPHERD.
Flag of Romania
ROMANIA HAS LOTS OF NATURAL GAS AND OIL.
Zagreb
ROMANIA
Galati
CARPETS MADE IN SARAJEVO.
LOCK ON THE RIVER DANUBE.
BLACK SEA
Flag of Yugoslavia
Belgrade
Bucharest
River Danube
Sarajevo
Varna
YUGOSLAVIA
BULGARIA
Flag of Bulgaria
TIMBER FROM FORESTS.
Sofia
GOLD CUPS ABOUT 2,000 YEARS OLD.
Plovdiv
European part of TURKEY
Istanbul
Tiranë
ALBANIA
ADRIATIC SEA
Flag of Albania
Thessaloniki
SUSPENSION BRIDGE IN ISTANBUL LINKING EUROPEAN TURKEY WITH ASIAN TURKEY.
Corfu
AEGEAN SEA
SORTING RAISINS WHICH ARE DRIED GRAPES.
GREECE
GREECE HAS A LARGE FLEET OF SHIPS WHICH CARRY GOODS FOR OTHER COUNTRIES.
Athens
MEDITERRANEAN SEA
Flag of Greece
Crete
Iraklion

Cherries and apricots are grown on the plains in Hungary. Most of the fruit is canned or made into jam.

Glass has been made in Czechoslovakia since the year 1300. Craftsmen cut beautiful patterns in the coloured glass.

This is a Polish cotton-spinning factory. Scientists are developing new machines for these factories.

Fields full of roses are grown in Bulgaria. They are used to make perfume. At rose-picking time, there is a festival.

Scandinavia

This group of countries is called Scandinavia. It is in the most northerly part of Europe.

There are only 22 million people in Scandinavia, which is about the same as in Tokyo, Japan. Each country has its own language. The Danish, Swedish and Norwegian languages are similar because they all come from a language called Old Norse. In Finland, some people speak Finnish and others speak Swedish.

The north of Scandinavia is very cold. For most of the year the land is covered with snow and ice. People called Lapps live there and keep reindeer.

Norway is very mountainous and its coastline is broken by tongues of deep water called fiords. Iceland is about 1,100 km from Norway. We have shown it closer so that it fits on the page.

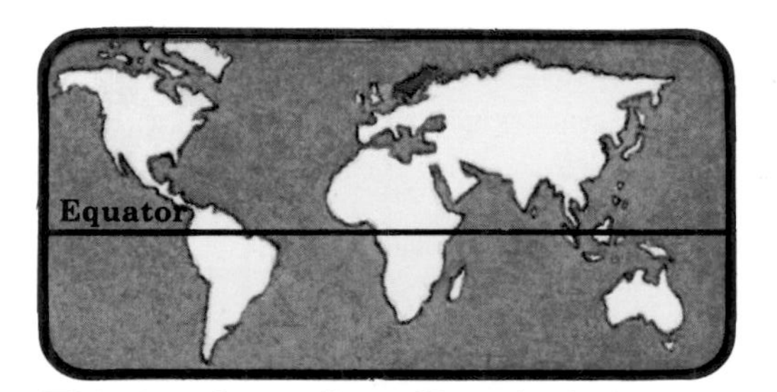
Equator

This is where Scandinavia is in the world.

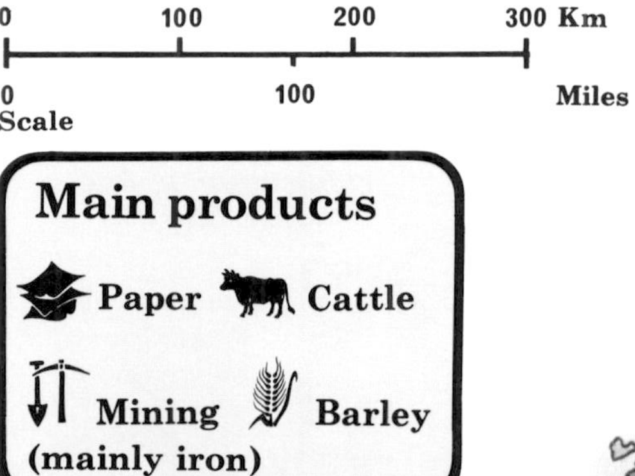
Main products
Paper
Cattle
Mining (mainly iron)
Barley

Fine porcelain is made in Denmark. The porcelain figures are often characters from Danish fairy tales like this little mermaid.

The sea between Finland and Sweden is frozen over in winter. Finland has a fleet of strongly built ships which can break through the ice.

0 100 200 300 Km
0 100 Miles
Scale
Tromsö
Narvik
Luleå
Oulu
IN THE COLD NORTH, PEOPLE CALLED LAPPS HERD REINDEER.
DRYING FISH SO THAT IT CAN BE KEPT.
THIS MAN CATCHES TINY GRAINS OF GOLD IN THE RIVER WATER.
DRILLING FOR IRON ORE IN AN UNDERGROUND MINE.
SAUNA BATHS WERE INVENTED IN FINLAND.
MUSK OX USED TO LIVE IN THE COLD NORTH.
FISHING IS A POPULAR SPORT IN SCANDINAVIA.
Flag of Finland
TRONDHEIM CATHEDRAL WAS BUILT 800 YEARS AGO. IT IS THE LARGEST CHURCH IN SCANDINAVIA.

Iceland
SHEEP SKINS ARE CLEANED TO MAKE RUGS AND COATS.
ICELAND
Reykjavik
Surtsey
Flag of Iceland

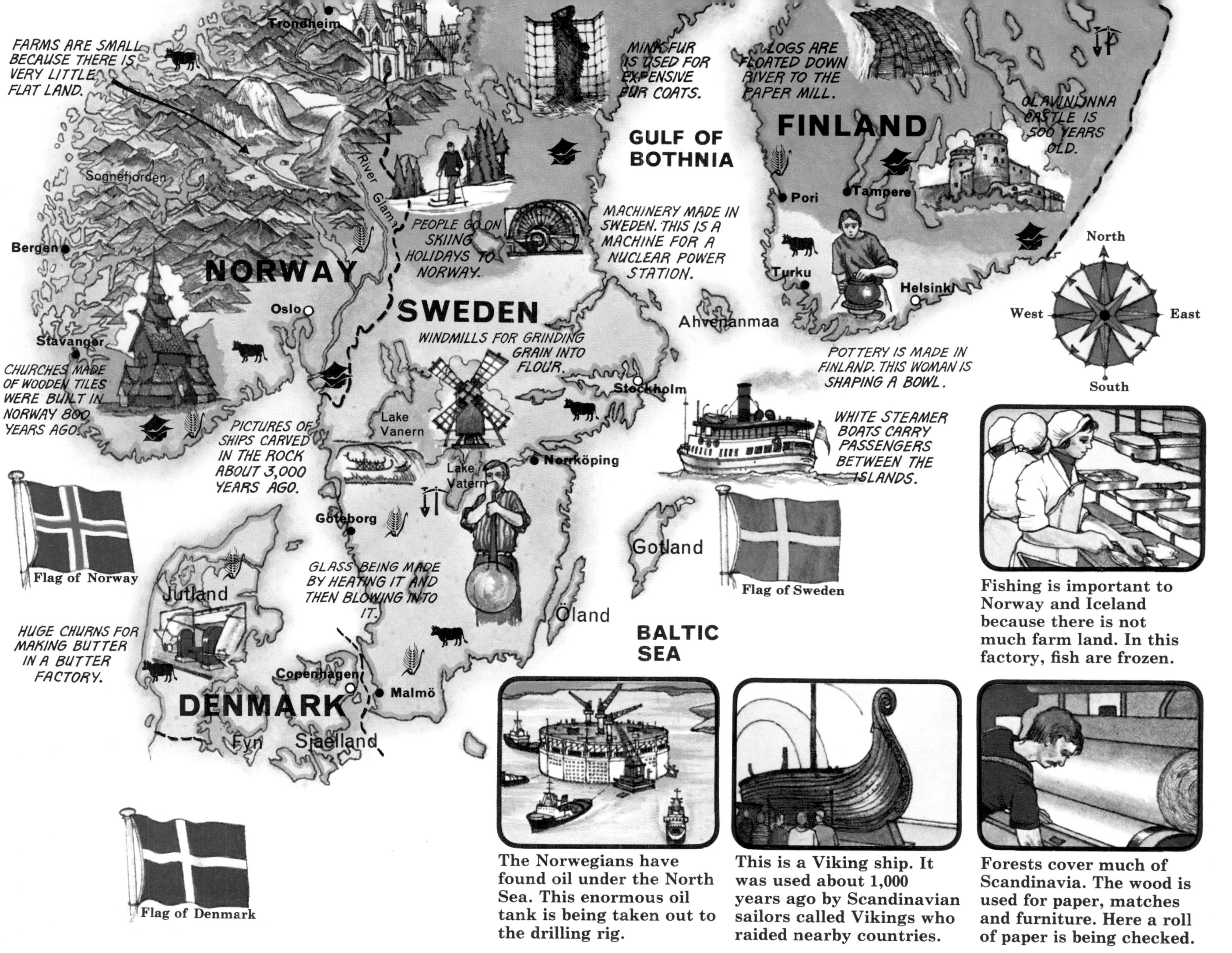
FARMS ARE SMALL BECAUSE THERE IS VERY LITTLE FLAT LAND.
Trondheim
Sognefjorden
River Glama
Bergen
NORWAY
Oslo
Stavanger
CHURCHES MADE OF WOODEN TILES WERE BUILT IN NORWAY 800 YEARS AGO.
PEOPLE GO ON SKIING HOLIDAYS TO NORWAY.
MINK FUR IS USED FOR EXPENSIVE FUR COATS.
GULF OF BOTHNIA
MACHINERY MADE IN SWEDEN. THIS IS A MACHINE FOR A NUCLEAR POWER STATION.
LOGS ARE FLOATED DOWN RIVER TO THE PAPER MILL.
FINLAND
OLAVINLINNA CASTLE IS 500 YEARS OLD.
Pori
Tampere
Turku
Helsinki
North
West
East
South
SWEDEN
WINDMILLS FOR GRINDING GRAIN INTO FLOUR.
Ahvenanmaa
POTTERY IS MADE IN FINLAND. THIS WOMAN IS SHAPING A BOWL.
Stockholm
Lake Vanern
Lake Vatern
Norrköping
PICTURES OF SHIPS CARVED IN THE ROCK ABOUT 3,000 YEARS AGO.
WHITE STEAMER BOATS CARRY PASSENGERS BETWEEN THE ISLANDS.
Göteborg
GLASS BEING MADE BY HEATING IT AND THEN BLOWING INTO IT.
Gotland
Flag of Norway
Flag of Sweden
Jutland
Öland
HUGE CHURNS FOR MAKING BUTTER IN A BUTTER FACTORY.
BALTIC SEA
Copenhagen
Malmö
DENMARK
Fyn
Sjaelland
Flag of Denmark

Fishing is important to Norway and Iceland because there is not much farm land. In this factory, fish are frozen.

The Norwegians have found oil under the North Sea. This enormous oil tank is being taken out to the drilling rig.

This is a Viking ship. It was used about 1,000 years ago by Scandinavian sailors called Vikings who raided nearby countries.

Forests cover much of Scandinavia. The wood is used for paper, matches and furniture. Here a roll of paper is being checked.

U.S.S.R.

People often call this area Russia, but its proper name is the Union of Soviet Socialist Republics, or U.S.S.R. for short. It is made up of 15 regions, or republics, and is the largest country in the world.

There are about 272 million people in the U.S.S.R. Three-quarters of them live in the west of the country. The north and the far east are bitterly cold for most of the year and few people live there.

Half the country is covered in thick forest. In the south it is warm enough to grow crops. All the farms and factories are owned by the government.

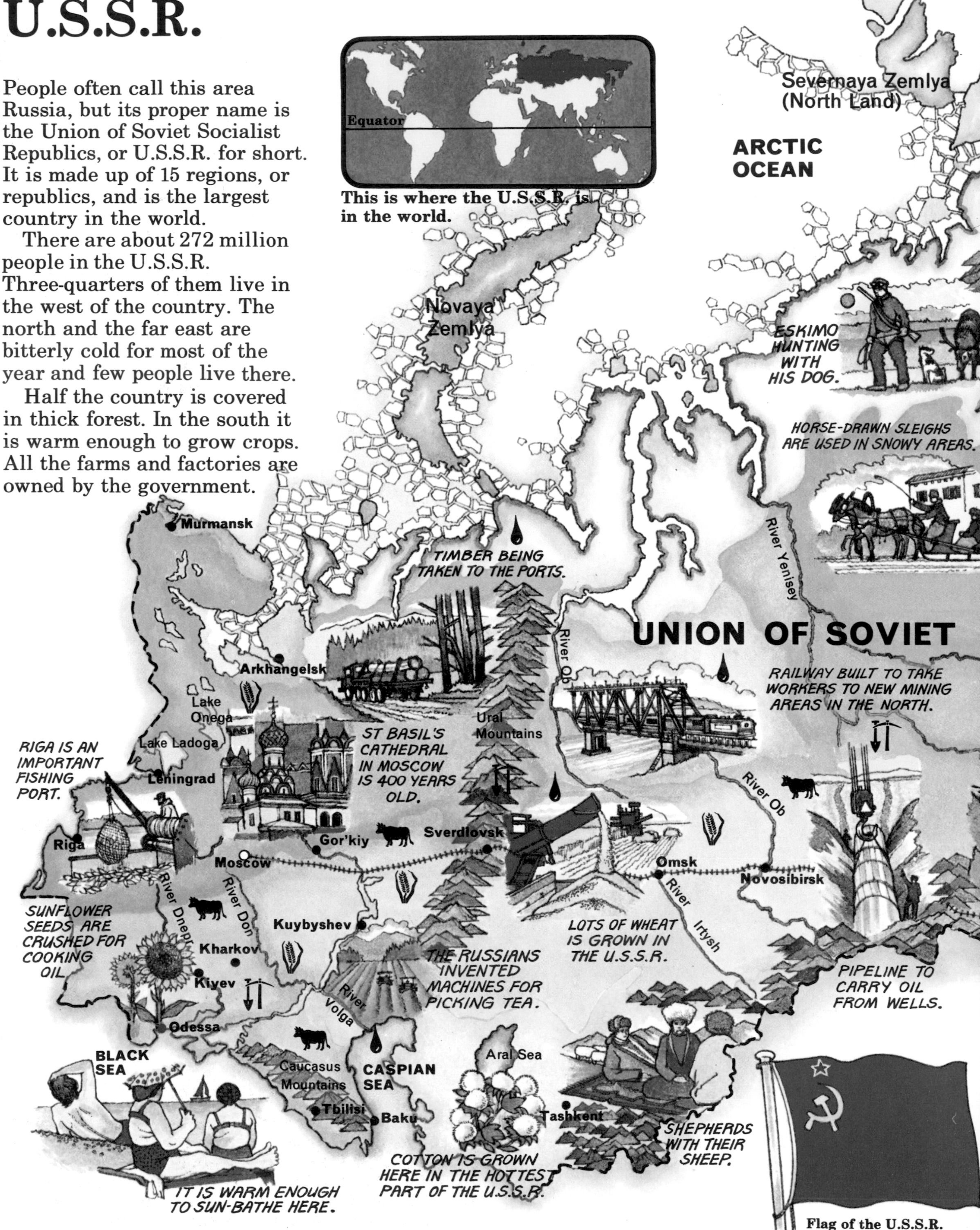

Equator
This is where the U.S.S.R. is in the world.
Severnaya Zemlya (North Land)
ARCTIC OCEAN
Novaya Zemlya
ESKIMO HUNTING WITH HIS DOG.
HORSE-DRAWN SLEIGHS ARE USED IN SNOWY AREAS.
River Yenisey
TIMBER BEING TAKEN TO THE PORTS.
UNION OF SOVIET
River Ob
RAILWAY BUILT TO TAKE WORKERS TO NEW MINING AREAS IN THE NORTH.
Murmansk
Arkhangelsk
Lake Onega
Lake Ladoga
Leningrad
Ural Mountains
ST BASIL'S CATHEDRAL IN MOSCOW IS 400 YEARS OLD.
RIGA IS AN IMPORTANT FISHING PORT.
Riga
Moscow
Gor'kiy
Sverdlovsk
Omsk
Novosibirsk
River Irtysh
River Dnepr
River Don
SUNFLOWER SEEDS ARE CRUSHED FOR COOKING OIL.
Kuybyshev
Kharkov
Kiyev
Odessa
LOTS OF WHEAT IS GROWN IN THE U.S.S.R.
THE RUSSIANS INVENTED MACHINES FOR PICKING TEA.
River Volga
PIPELINE TO CARRY OIL FROM WELLS.
BLACK SEA
Caucasus Mountains
CASPIAN SEA
Aral Sea
Tbilisi
Baku
Tashkent
SHEPHERDS WITH THEIR SHEEP.
COTTON IS GROWN HERE IN THE HOTTEST PART OF THE U.S.S.R.
IT IS WARM ENOUGH TO SUN-BATHE HERE.

Flag of the U.S.S.R.

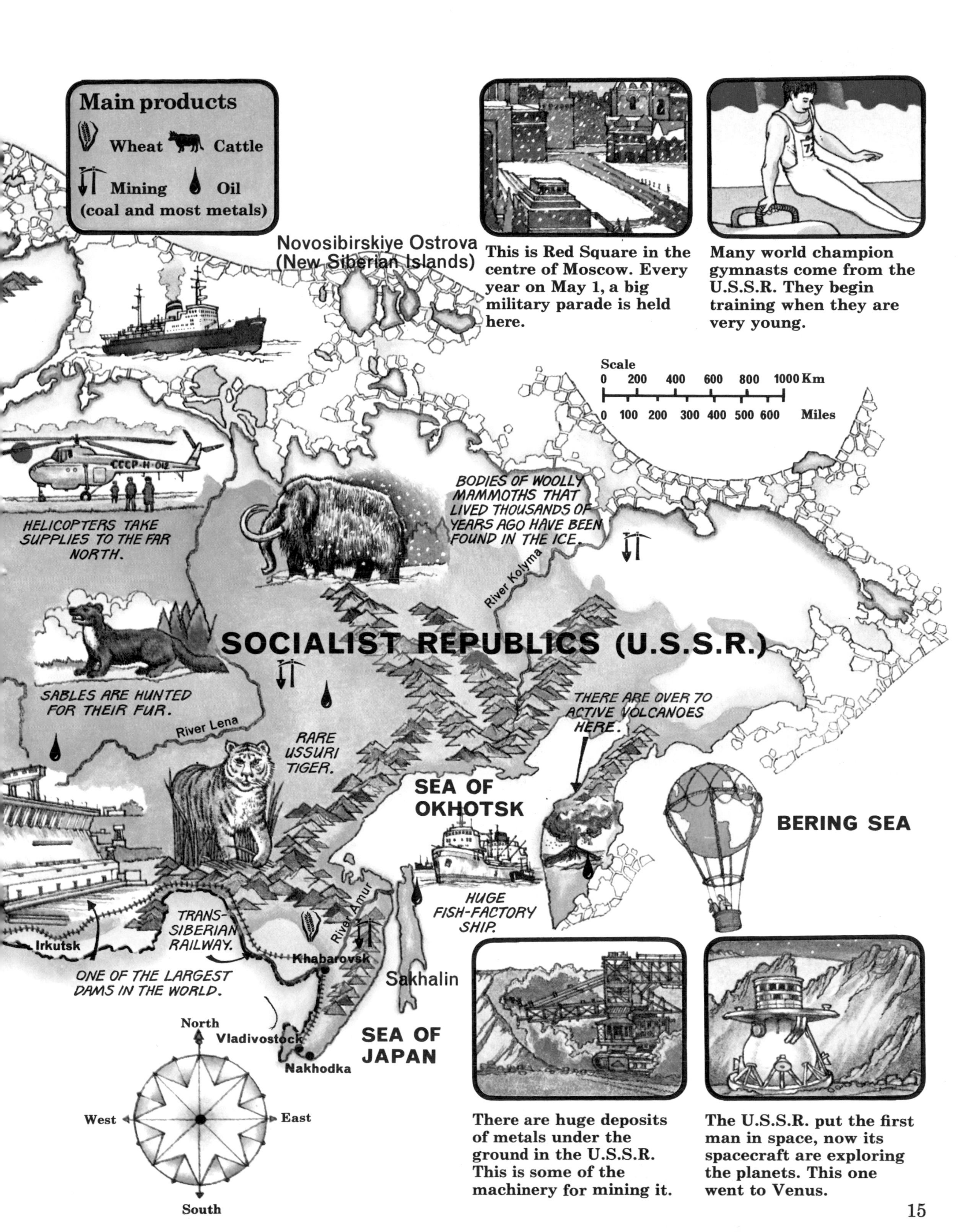
Main products
Wheat
Cattle
Mining
Oil
(coal and most metals)
Novosibirskiye Ostrova
(New Siberian Islands)
Scale
0 200 400 600 800 1000 Km
0 100 200 300 400 500 600 Miles
CCCP-H-012
HELICOPTERS TAKE SUPPLIES TO THE FAR NORTH.
BODIES OF WOOLLY MAMMOTHS THAT LIVED THOUSANDS OF YEARS AGO HAVE BEEN FOUND IN THE ICE.
River Kolyma
SOCIALIST REPUBLICS (U.S.S.R.)
SABLES ARE HUNTED FOR THEIR FUR.
River Lena
RARE USSURI TIGER.
THERE ARE OVER 70 ACTIVE VOLCANOES HERE.
SEA OF OKHOTSK
BERING SEA
HUGE FISH-FACTORY SHIP.
TRANS-SIBERIAN RAILWAY.
River Amur
Irkutsk
Khabarovsk
ONE OF THE LARGEST DAMS IN THE WORLD.
Sakhalin
North
Vladivostock
Nakhodka
SEA OF JAPAN
West
East
South

This is Red Square in the centre of Moscow. Every year on May 1, a big military parade is held here.

Many world champion gymnasts come from the U.S.S.R. They begin training when they are very young.

There are huge deposits of metals under the ground in the U.S.S.R. This is some of the machinery for mining it.

The U.S.S.R. put the first man in space, now its spacecraft are exploring the planets. This one went to Venus.

Middle East

The Middle East is part of Asia. Nearly a third of the land is hot, sun-scorched desert. Very little grows in the desert because it is so dry.

The valleys of the Tigris and Euphrates rivers are good for farming. River water is used for watering the crops because there is not much rain. In Israel, lots of oranges, lemons and grapefruit are grown.

The city of Jerusalem is holy to followers of the Jewish, Christian and Islam religions. All three religions have holy buildings in the city where people go to pray.

There are four main languages in this area. Turkish is spoken in Turkey and Persian in Iran. In Israel, people speak Hebrew, and in the rest of the countries Arabic is spoken.

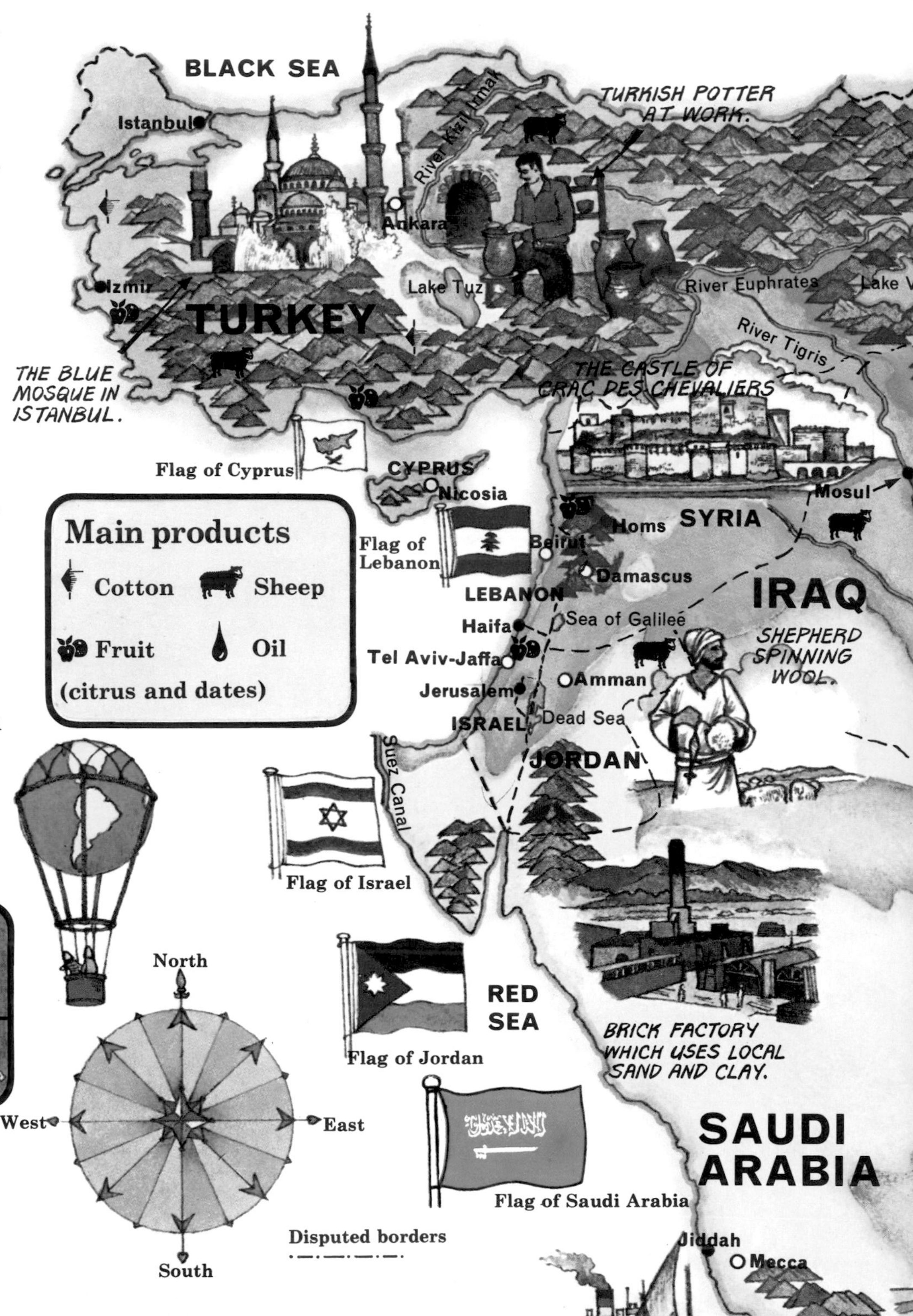

BLACK SEA
Istanbul
Ankara
Izmir
TURKEY
Lake Tuz
River Kizil Irmak
TURKISH POTTER AT WORK.
River Euphrates
Lake V
River Tigris
THE BLUE MOSQUE IN ISTANBUL.
THE CASTLE OF CRAC DES CHEVALIERS
Flag of Cyprus
CYPRUS
Nicosia
Mosul
SYRIA
Homs
Main products
Cotton
Sheep
Fruit (citrus and dates)
Oil
Flag of Lebanon
Beirut
Damascus
LEBANON
IRAQ
Haifa
Sea of Galilee
SHEPHERD SPINNING WOOL.
Tel Aviv-Jaffa
Amman
Jerusalem
ISRAEL
Dead Sea
JORDAN
Suez Canal
Flag of Israel
North
West
East
South
Flag of Jordan
RED SEA
BRICK FACTORY WHICH USES LOCAL SAND AND CLAY.
SAUDI ARABIA
Flag of Saudi Arabia
Disputed borders
Jiddah
Mecca
SMALL SAILING SHIPS CALLED DHOWS BRING SUPPLIES FROM LARGE SHIPS.

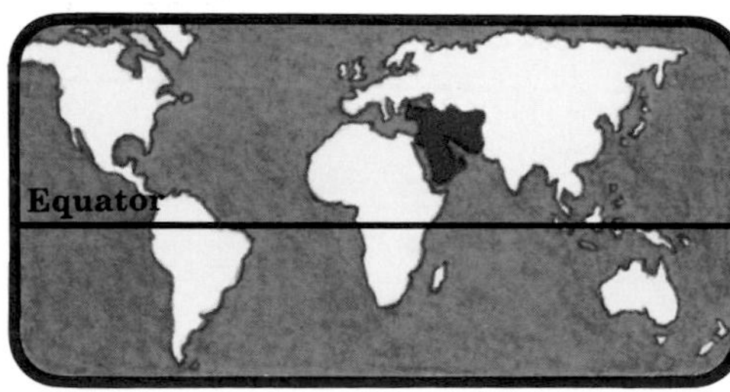

Equator

This is where the Middle East is in the world.

Scale

0	100	200	300	400	500	600	Km
0	100	200	300				Miles

This is a factory for packing dried dates. Date palms grow in hot, dry places. Most of the world's dates come from Iraq.

This machinery in the desert is part of an oil well. Huge amounts of oil have been found under the ground in the desert.

This is the Dome of the Rock in Jerusalem. It is a mosque where followers of the Islam religion pray several times every day.

Flag of North Yemen

Flag of Turkey
Flag of Syria
CAVIAR—EGGS OF THE STURGEON FISH—COMES FROM IRAN.
CASPIAN SEA
FACTORY WHERE PLASTICS ARE MADE FROM OIL.
Flag of Iran
Flag of Iraq
Rasht
Lake Urmiyeh
Mashhad
Tehran
Kirkuk
IRAN
Baghdad
Esfahan
WOOL AND COTTON FACTORY.
ANCIENT TOWN OF PERSEPOLIS.
NEW WATERING SYSTEMS HAVE MADE FARMING POSSIBLE HERE.
Basra
Abadan
KUWAIT
Kuwait
Flag of Kuwait
Flag of Bahrain
WATER TOWERS IN THE DESERT.
BAHRAIN
QATAR
Doha
Dubai
Abu Dhabi
Flag of Qatar
Riyadh
Flag of United Arab Emirates
Muscat
BEDOUIN TRIBESMEN ROAM THE DESERT.
UNITED ARAB EMIRATES
OMAN
ARABIAN ORYX.
FISHERMEN SORTING THE DAY'S CATCH.
DESERT TRIBESPEOPLE BUILD TEMPORARY SHELTERS AGAINST THE SUN AND WIND.
SOUTH YEMEN
NORTH YEMEN
Flag of Oman
ARABIAN SEA
WEIGHING RAW COTTON.
San'a
KUWAITI BOOM SHIP RETURNING FROM AFRICA.
Flag of South Yemen
Socotra
Aden

In Israel, many people live and work together in villages called kibbutzim. Israel is a new country which was made in 1948.

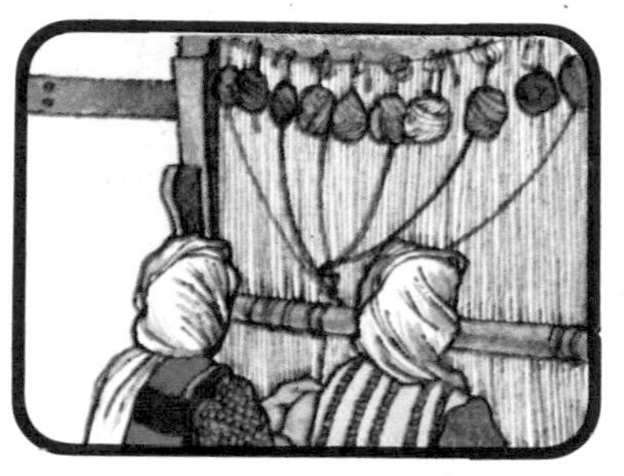

These Turkish women are weaving a carpet from brightly coloured wools. Very beautiful carpets are also made in Iran.

Shoes are being made in this factory in Saudi Arabia. Many craftsmen still make shoes in street workshops.

It is the custom for women to wear veils to hide their faces. Many women have given up the veil and now wear modern clothes.

Africa

There are about 535 million people in Africa and over 800 different languages are spoken. It is the homeland of the Negro peoples, though about five million Europeans live there too.

The weather is very hot and rainy near the equator. South of the equator there is less rain and the land is covered with tall grass which shrivels and dies in the dry season. Lions, zebras, giraffes and elephants live in these grasslands.

North of the equator is the Sahara desert, which is the largest desert in the world. It is so dry that people live only where there is a well or an oasis pool.

Until recently, most of Africa was ruled by European countries. Now the African people are making and ruling their own countries.

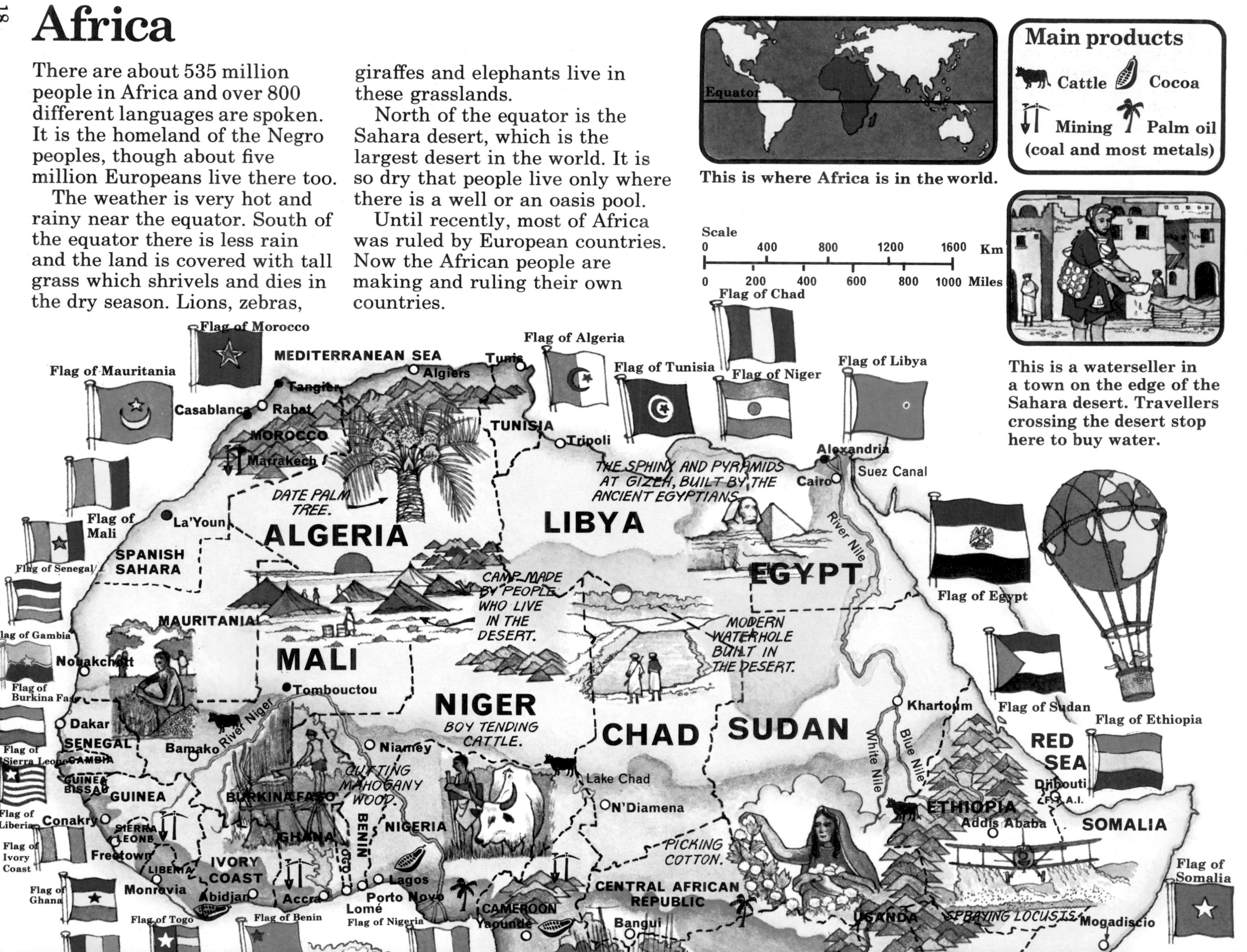
Equator
This is where Africa is in the world.
Main products
Cattle
Cocoa
Mining
Palm oil
(coal and most metals)
Scale
0 400 800 1200 1600 Km
0 200 400 600 800 1000 Miles
This is a waterseller in a town on the edge of the Sahara desert. Travellers crossing the desert stop here to buy water.
Flag of Morocco
Flag of Mauritania
Flag of Algeria
Flag of Tunisia
Flag of Chad
Flag of Niger
Flag of Libya
Flag of Mali
Flag of Senegal
Flag of Gambia
Flag of Burkina Faso
Flag of Sierra Leone
Flag of Liberia
Flag of Ivory Coast
Flag of Ghana
Flag of Togo
Flag of Benin
Flag of Nigeria
Flag of Egypt
Flag of Sudan
Flag of Ethiopia
Flag of Somalia
MEDITERRANEAN SEA
Tangier
Casablanca
Rabat
Algiers
Tunis
MOROCCO
Marrakech
TUNISIA
Tripoli
Alexandria
Suez Canal
Cairo
THE SPHINX AND PYRAMIDS AT GIZEH, BUILT BY THE ANCIENT EGYPTIANS.
DATE PALM TREE.
La'Youn
ALGERIA
LIBYA
River Nile
SPANISH SAHARA
EGYPT
CAMP MADE BY PEOPLE WHO LIVE IN THE DESERT.
MAURITANIA
MALI
MODERN WATERHOLE BUILT IN THE DESERT.
Nouakchott
Tombouctou
NIGER
BOY TENDING CATTLE.
Khartoum
Dakar
SENEGAL
GAMBIA
GUINEA BISSAU
GUINEA
Bamako
River Niger
Niamey
CHAD
SUDAN
RED SEA
White Nile
Blue Nile
CUTTING MAHOGANY WOOD.
Lake Chad
N'Diamena
Djibouti
F.T.A.I.
BURKINA FASO
ETHIOPIA
Addis Ababa
SOMALIA
Conakry
SIERRA LEONE
Freetown
LIBERIA
Monrovia
IVORY COAST
Abidjan
GHANA
Accra
TOGO
Lomé
BENIN
Porto Novo
NIGERIA
Lagos
PICKING COTTON.
CENTRAL AFRICAN REPUBLIC
Bangui
CAMEROON
Yaounde
UGANDA
SPRAYING LOCUSTS.
Mogadiscio

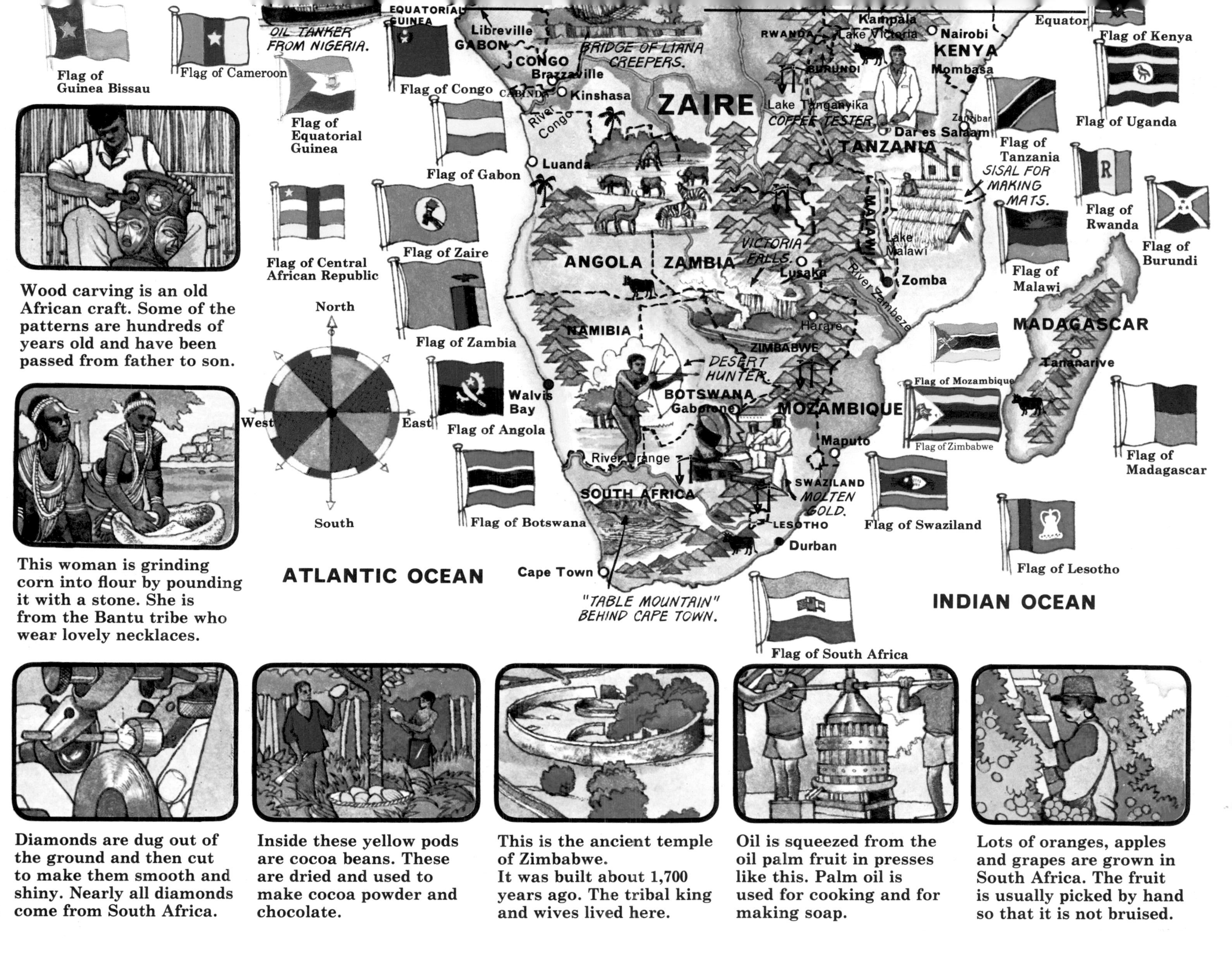

Flag of Guinea Bissau
Flag of Cameroon
OIL TANKER FROM NIGERIA.
EQUATORIAL GUINEA
Flag of Equatorial Guinea
Flag of Congo
Libreville
GABON
CONGO
Brazzaville
CABINDA
Kinshasa
River Congo
BRIDGE OF LIANA CREEPERS.
ZAIRE
Flag of Gabon
Luanda
Flag of Central African Republic
Flag of Zaire
ANGOLA
ZAMBIA
Flag of Zambia
NAMIBIA
North
South
East
West
Walvis Bay
Flag of Angola
Flag of Botswana
BOTSWANA
Gaborone
DESERT HUNTER.
River Orange
SOUTH AFRICA
Cape Town
"TABLE MOUNTAIN" BEHIND CAPE TOWN.
ATLANTIC OCEAN
RWANDA
BURUNDI
Kampala
Lake Victoria
Nairobi
KENYA
Mombasa
Lake Tanganyika
COFFEE TESTER.
Zanzibar
Dar es Salaam
TANZANIA
MALAWI
Lake Malawi
Zomba
River Zambeze
VICTORIA FALLS.
Lusaka
Harare
ZIMBABWE
MOZAMBIQUE
Maputo
SWAZILAND
MOLTEN GOLD.
LESOTHO
Durban
Equator
Flag of Kenya
Flag of Uganda
Flag of Tanzania
SISAL FOR MAKING MATS.
Flag of Rwanda
Flag of Burundi
Flag of Malawi
MADAGASCAR
Tananarive
Flag of Mozambique
Flag of Zimbabwe
Flag of Madagascar
Flag of Swaziland
Flag of Lesotho
Flag of South Africa
INDIAN OCEAN

Wood carving is an old African craft. Some of the patterns are hundreds of years old and have been passed from father to son.

This woman is grinding corn into flour by pounding it with a stone. She is from the Bantu tribe who wear lovely necklaces.

Diamonds are dug out of the ground and then cut to make them smooth and shiny. Nearly all diamonds come from South Africa.

Inside these yellow pods are cocoa beans. These are dried and used to make cocoa powder and chocolate.

This is the ancient temple of Zimbabwe.
It was built about 1,700 years ago. The tribal king and wives lived here.

Oil is squeezed from the oil palm fruit in presses like this. Palm oil is used for cooking and for making soap.

Lots of oranges, apples and grapes are grown in South Africa. The fruit is usually picked by hand so that it is not bruised.

Asia 1

This map shows the central part of Asia. The Himalayan region in the north is cool and the mountains are covered with snow. As you travel down towards Sri Lanka, the climate gets hotter and more tropical.

From June until September there are heavy rains, called monsoons. These are followed by eight months of very hot dry weather.

990 million people live in this part of Asia. Many of them live next to rivers or the sea because these places are coolest. The River Ganges valley is one of the most thickly populated places in the world.

Most of the people work in the fields growing food, though farming is made difficult by the climate.

The main languages in India and Pakistan are Hindi and Urdu.

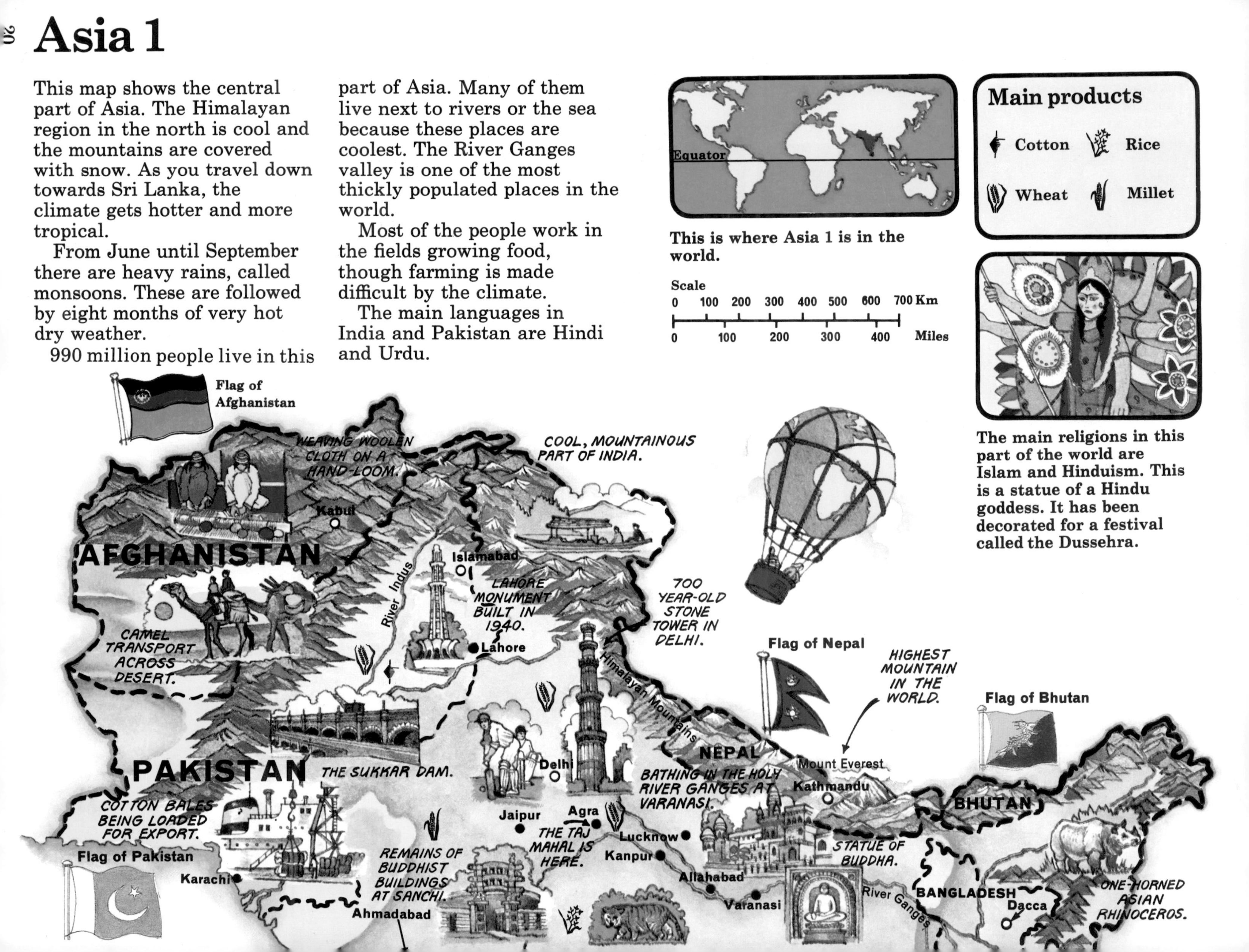
Equator
This is where Asia 1 is in the world.
Scale
0 100 200 300 400 500 600 700 Km
0 100 200 300 400 Miles
Main products
Cotton
Rice
Wheat
Millet
The main religions in this part of the world are Islam and Hinduism. This is a statue of a Hindu goddess. It has been decorated for a festival called the Dussehra.
Flag of Afghanistan
WEAVING WOOLEN CLOTH ON A HAND-LOOM.
Kabul
AFGHANISTAN
CAMEL TRANSPORT ACROSS DESERT.
COOL, MOUNTAINOUS PART OF INDIA.
Islamabad
River Indus
LAHORE MONUMENT BUILT IN 1940.
Lahore
700 YEAR-OLD STONE TOWER IN DELHI.
Himalayan Mountains
Flag of Nepal
HIGHEST MOUNTAIN IN THE WORLD.
Mount Everest
Kathmandu
NEPAL
Flag of Bhutan
BHUTAN
PAKISTAN
THE SUKKAR DAM.
COTTON BALES BEING LOADED FOR EXPORT.
Flag of Pakistan
Karachi
Delhi
Jaipur
Agra
THE TAJ MAHAL IS HERE.
BATHING IN THE HOLY RIVER GANGES AT VARANASI.
Lucknow
Kanpur
Allahabad
Varanasi
STATUE OF BUDDHA.
River Ganges
REMAINS OF BUDDHIST BUILDINGS AT SANCHI.
Ahmadabad
BANGLADESH
Dacca
ONE-HORNED ASIAN RHINOCEROS.

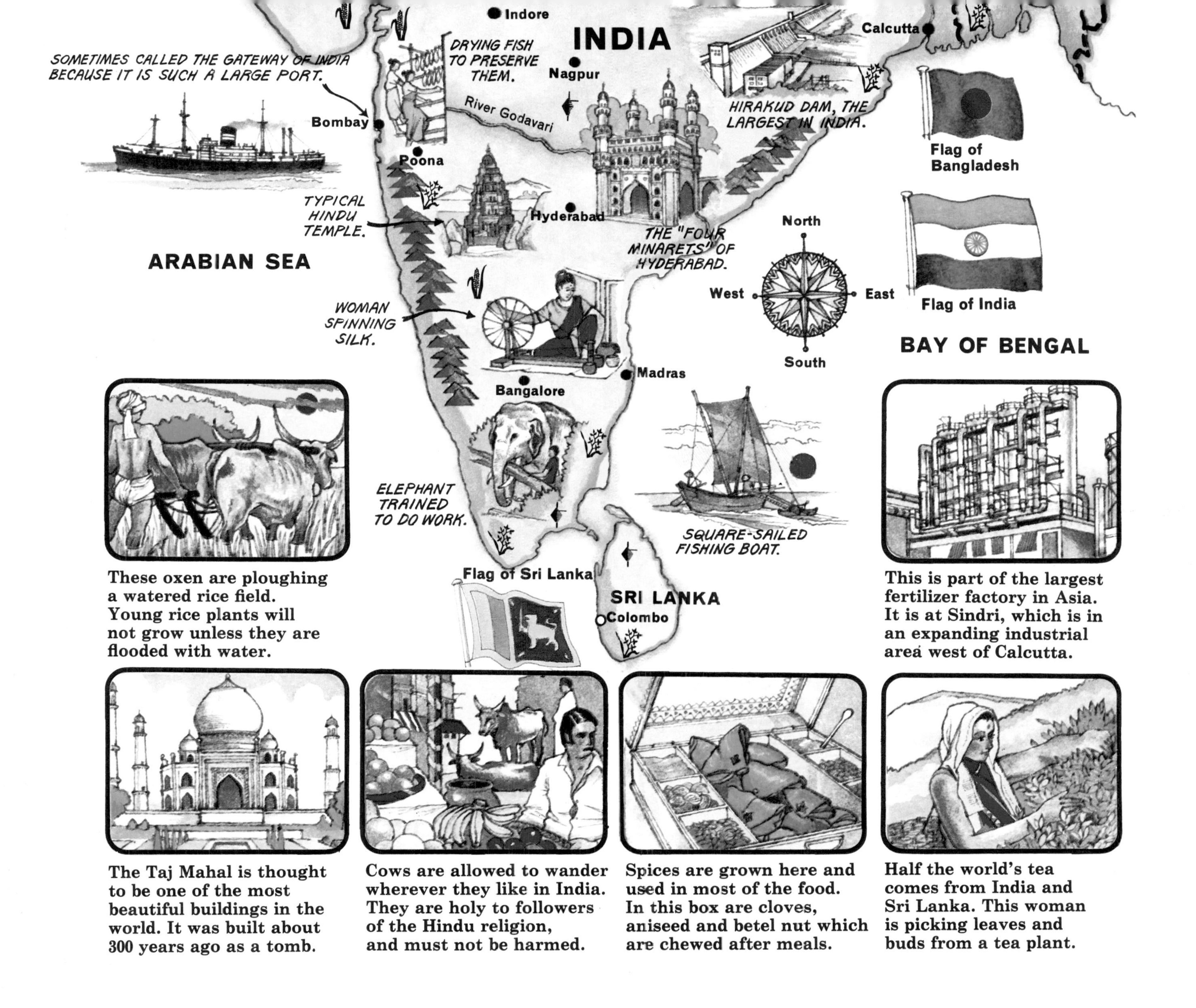
INDIA
Indore
Calcutta
SOMETIMES CALLED THE GATEWAY OF INDIA BECAUSE IT IS SUCH A LARGE PORT.
DRYING FISH TO PRESERVE THEM.
Nagpur
Bombay
River Godavari
HIRAKUD DAM, THE LARGEST IN INDIA.
Flag of Bangladesh
Poona
TYPICAL HINDU TEMPLE.
Hyderabad
THE "FOUR MINARETS" OF HYDERABAD.
North
West
East
South
Flag of India
ARABIAN SEA
WOMAN SPINNING SILK.
BAY OF BENGAL
Madras
Bangalore
ELEPHANT TRAINED TO DO WORK.
SQUARE-SAILED FISHING BOAT.
Flag of Sri Lanka
SRI LANKA
Colombo

These oxen are ploughing a watered rice field. Young rice plants will not grow unless they are flooded with water.

This is part of the largest fertilizer factory in Asia. It is at Sindri, which is in an expanding industrial area west of Calcutta.

The Taj Mahal is thought to be one of the most beautiful buildings in the world. It was built about 300 years ago as a tomb.

Cows are allowed to wander wherever they like in India. They are holy to followers of the Hindu religion, and must not be harmed.

Spices are grown here and used in most of the food. In this box are cloves, aniseed and betel nut which are chewed after meals.

Half the world's tea comes from India and Sri Lanka. This woman is picking leaves and buds from a tea plant.

Asia 2

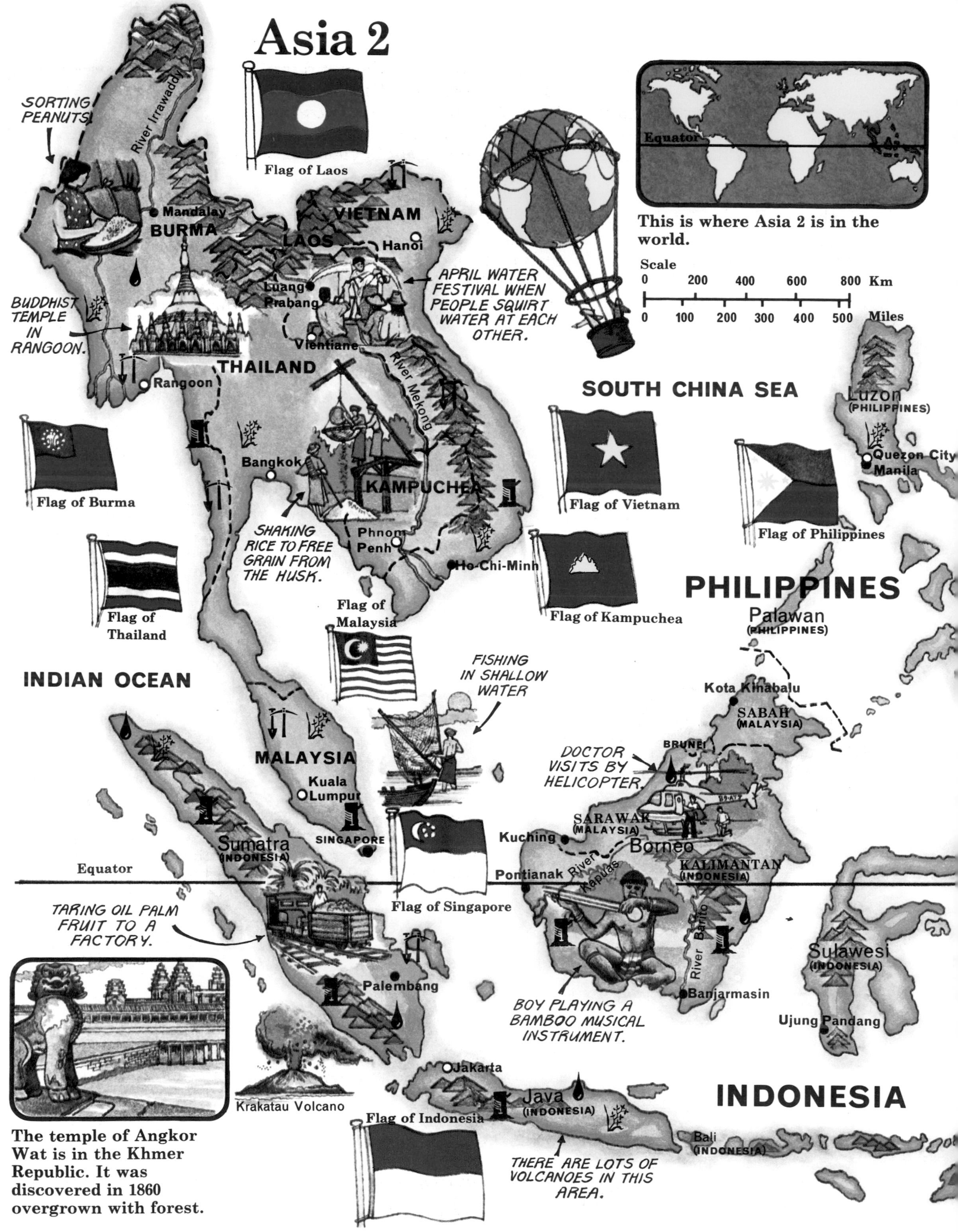

Flag of Laos
Equator
Scale
0 200 400 600 800 Km
0 100 200 300 400 500 Miles
SORTING PEANUTS
River Irrawaddy
Mandalay
BURMA
VIETNAM
LAOS
Hanoi
APRIL WATER FESTIVAL WHEN PEOPLE SQUIRT WATER AT EACH OTHER.
Luang Prabang
BUDDHIST TEMPLE IN RANGOON.
Vientiane
THAILAND
Rangoon
River Mekong
SOUTH CHINA SEA
Luzon (PHILIPPINES)
Flag of Burma
Bangkok
KAMPUCHEA
Flag of Vietnam
Quezon City
Manila
Flag of Philippines
SHAKING RICE TO FREE GRAIN FROM THE HUSK.
Phnom Penh
Ho-Chi-Minh
Flag of Thailand
Flag of Kampuchea
PHILIPPINES
Palawan (PHILIPPINES)
Flag of Malaysia
INDIAN OCEAN
FISHING IN SHALLOW WATER
Kota Kinabalu
SABAH (MALAYSIA)
BRUNEI
MALAYSIA
DOCTOR VISITS BY HELICOPTER.
Kuala Lumpur
SARAWAK (MALAYSIA)
Sumatra (INDONESIA)
SINGAPORE
Kuching
Borneo
KALIMANTAN (INDONESIA)
Equator
Pontianak
River Kapuas
TAKING OIL PALM FRUIT TO A FACTORY.
Flag of Singapore
River Barito
Sulawesi (INDONESIA)
Palembang
Banjarmasin
BOY PLAYING A BAMBOO MUSICAL INSTRUMENT.
Ujung Pandang
Jakarta
Java (INDONESIA)
INDONESIA
Krakatau Volcano
Flag of Indonesia
Bali (INDONESIA)
THERE ARE LOTS OF VOLCANOES IN THIS AREA.

This is where Asia 2 is in the world.

The temple of Angkor Wat is in the Khmer Republic. It was discovered in 1860 overgrown with forest.

These countries are known as South-East Asia. Like other places on the equator they have hot, wet weather. For several months there are torrential rains called monsoons.

Lush, green rain forest grows in all the countries. Some of the trees, such as teak and mahogany, are cut down for their beautiful wood. Monkeys, tigers, leopards and brightly-coloured birds live in the forest.

The forest has to be cut down to make farmland. Rice, rubber trees and coconuts are grown. Round the islands, fishermen catch sardines, anchovies and tuna fish.

The Philippines and Indonesia are countries made up of several islands. There are about 416 million people in South-East Asia. Over a third of them live in Indonesia, but some of the islands have no people at all.

In Malaysia, tin is washed out of the rocks with fierce jets of water. Malaysia is the world's leading producer of tin.

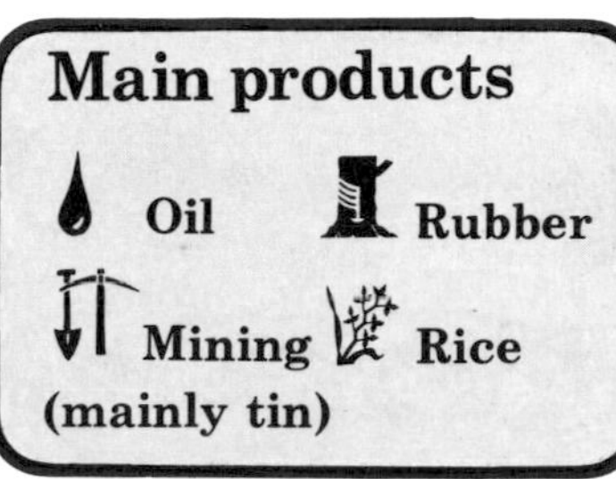
Main products
Oil
Rubber
Mining (mainly tin)
Rice

Elephants are trained to do heavy work. They are useful for moving logs in the rain forest where there are no roads for lorries.

This man is splitting coconuts open. Oil from the white flesh of the coconut is used to make cooking oils and candles.

This is patterned cloth called batik. It is made by drawing patterns with wax and then dying the cloth. The waxed parts are not coloured by the dye and so leave a pattern on the cloth.

This is a rubber tree plantation. Rubber is made from latex which trickles out of cuts made in the bark of the rubber trees. This man is collecting the latex.

Bangkok has a network of canals called klongs. On one of these there is a floating market where fruit and vegetables are sold from boats.

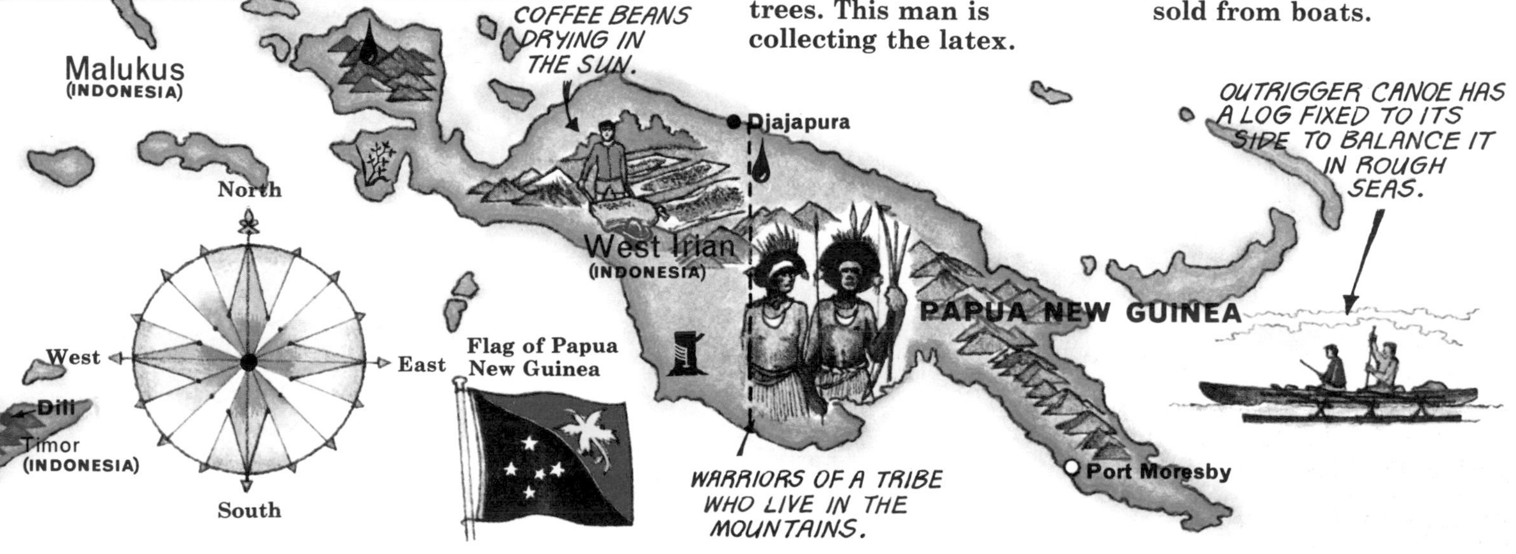
Malaku
(PHILIPPINES)
Davao
PACIFIC OCEAN
Manado
Equator
COFFEE BEANS DRYING IN THE SUN.
Malukus
(INDONESIA)
Djajapura
OUTRIGGER CANOE HAS A LOG FIXED TO ITS SIDE TO BALANCE IT IN ROUGH SEAS.
North
West Irian
(INDONESIA)
PAPUA NEW GUINEA
West
East
Flag of Papua New Guinea
Dili
Timor
(INDONESIA)
South
WARRIORS OF A TRIBE WHO LIVE IN THE MOUNTAINS.
Port Moresby

Asia 3

There are over 1,000 million people in this part of Asia. China has more people than any other country in the world. Most of them live in eastern China.

South of the River Yangtze the weather is very hot and in summer there are heavy monsoon rains. This is where most of China's rice is grown.

Not all deserts are hot. The Gobi desert in Mongolia is very dry and bare, but it is bitterly cold for most of the year.

Each country in this area has its own language. In China, several types of Chinese are spoken, but most people speak Mandarin Chinese. Chinese writing uses very simple pictures, called characters, instead of alphabet letters.

Main products

Rice · Oil · Mining (mainly coal) · Tea

Scale

0 100 200 300 400 500 600 700 Km

0 100 200 300 400 Miles

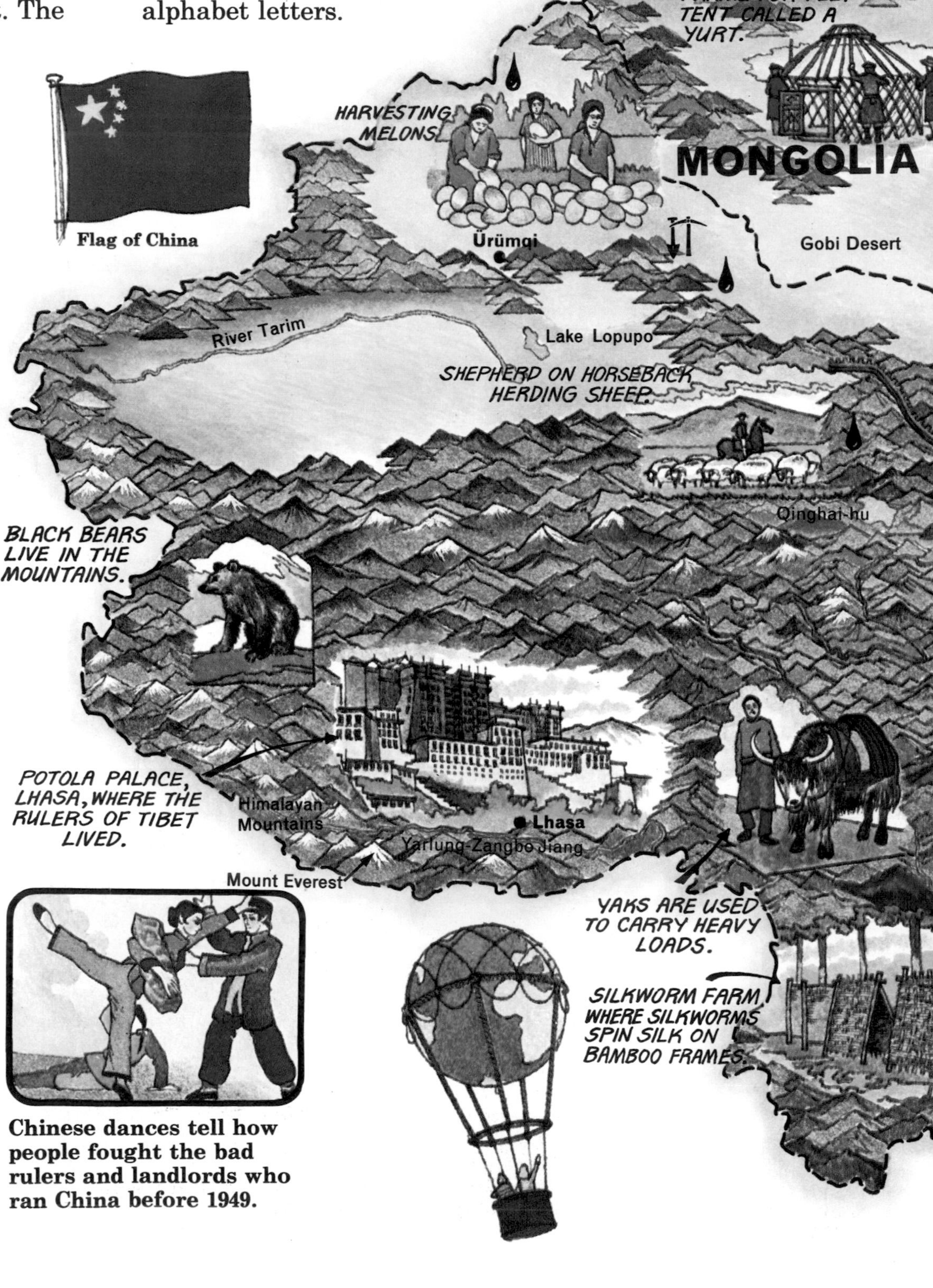

Flag of China
FRAME FOR FELT TENT CALLED A YURT.
HARVESTING MELONS
MONGOLIA
Ürümqi
Gobi Desert
River Tarim
Lake Lopupo
SHEPHERD ON HORSEBACK HERDING SHEEP.
Qinghai-hu
BLACK BEARS LIVE IN THE MOUNTAINS.
POTOLA PALACE, LHASA, WHERE THE RULERS OF TIBET LIVED.
Himalayan Mountains
Lhasa
Yarlung-Zangbo Jiang
Mount Everest
YAKS ARE USED TO CARRY HEAVY LOADS.
SILKWORM FARM, WHERE SILKWORMS SPIN SILK ON BAMBOO FRAMES.

This is a furnace for melting steel. The Chinese work together in groups called communes, sharing tools and profits.

This is Hong Kong. It is a tiny part of China which is on loan to Britain for 99 years until the year 1997.

The Great Wall of China is 2,400 km long. It was built about 1,500 years ago to protect China from attack by enemies.

Chinese dances tell how people fought the bad rulers and landlords who ran China before 1949.

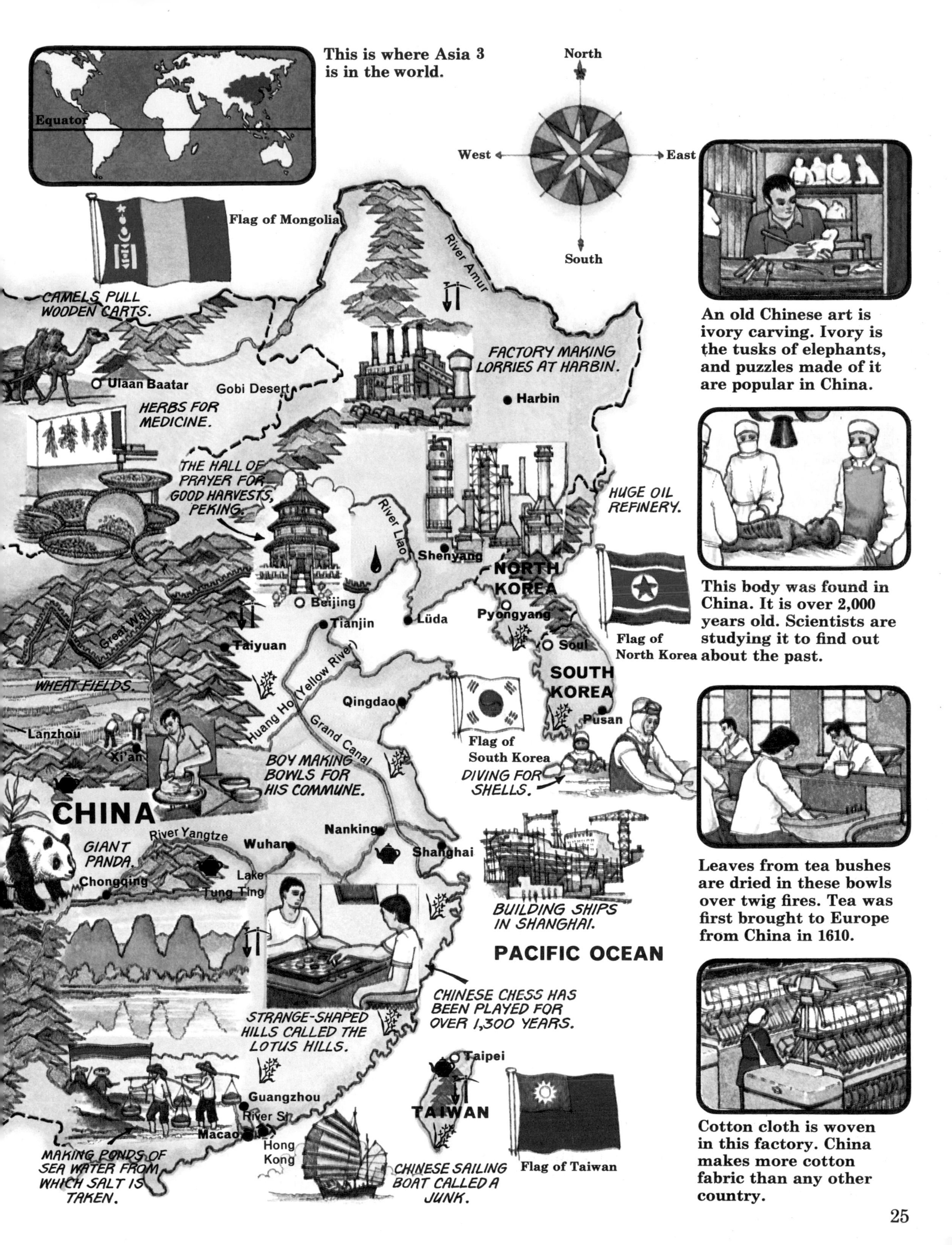

This is where Asia 3 is in the world.
Equator
North
West
East
South
Flag of Mongolia
CAMELS PULL WOODEN CARTS.
Ulaan Baatar
Gobi Desert
HERBS FOR MEDICINE.
River Amur
FACTORY MAKING LORRIES AT HARBIN.
Harbin
THE HALL OF PRAYER FOR GOOD HARVESTS, PEKING.
River Liao
HUGE OIL REFINERY.
Shenyang
NORTH KOREA
Beijing
Tianjin
Lüda
Pyongyang
Great Wall
Taiyuan
Soul
Flag of North Korea
Huang Ho (Yellow River)
SOUTH KOREA
WHEAT FIELDS.
Qingdao
Grand Canal
Pusan
Lanzhou
Xi'an
Flag of South Korea
BOY MAKING BOWLS FOR HIS COMMUNE.
DIVING FOR SHELLS.
CHINA
River Yangtze
Nanking
GIANT PANDA.
Wuhan
Shanghai
Lake Tung Ting
Chongqing
BUILDING SHIPS IN SHANGHAI.
PACIFIC OCEAN
CHINESE CHESS HAS BEEN PLAYED FOR OVER 1,300 YEARS.
STRANGE-SHAPED HILLS CALLED THE LOTUS HILLS.
Taipei
Guangzhou
TAIWAN
River Si
Macao
Hong Kong
MAKING PONDS OF SEA WATER FROM WHICH SALT IS TAKEN.
CHINESE SAILING BOAT CALLED A JUNK.
Flag of Taiwan

An old Chinese art is ivory carving. Ivory is the tusks of elephants, and puzzles made of it are popular in China.

This body was found in China. It is over 2,000 years old. Scientists are studying it to find out about the past.

Leaves from tea bushes are dried in these bowls over twig fires. Tea was first brought to Europe from China in 1610.

Cotton cloth is woven in this factory. China makes more cotton fabric than any other country.

Japan

Japan is made up of four main islands. It is cold there in winter, hot in summer and warm in spring and autumn. There is also a rainy season in June, and in September there are sometimes dangerously strong winds, or typhoons.

More than 120 million people live in Japan, most of them in the cities.
Yokohama have now grown into one vast city, which has more people in it than any other city in the world.

Until about 100 years ago, Japan was cut off from the rest of the world. Very few foreigners were allowed in. Modern industry began there only about 20 years ago. Japan is now one of the world's leading industrial countries.

Equator

This is where Japan is in the world.

0 100 200 300 Km

Scale 0 100 Miles

Main products

- **Rice**
- **Motorcycles**
- **Fruit (apples and oranges)**
- **Light machinery**

The world's first high-speed train was built in Japan. It can travel at 149 m.p.h. (240 k.p.h.). The line passes Mt Fuji, an old volcano which is holy to the Japanese.

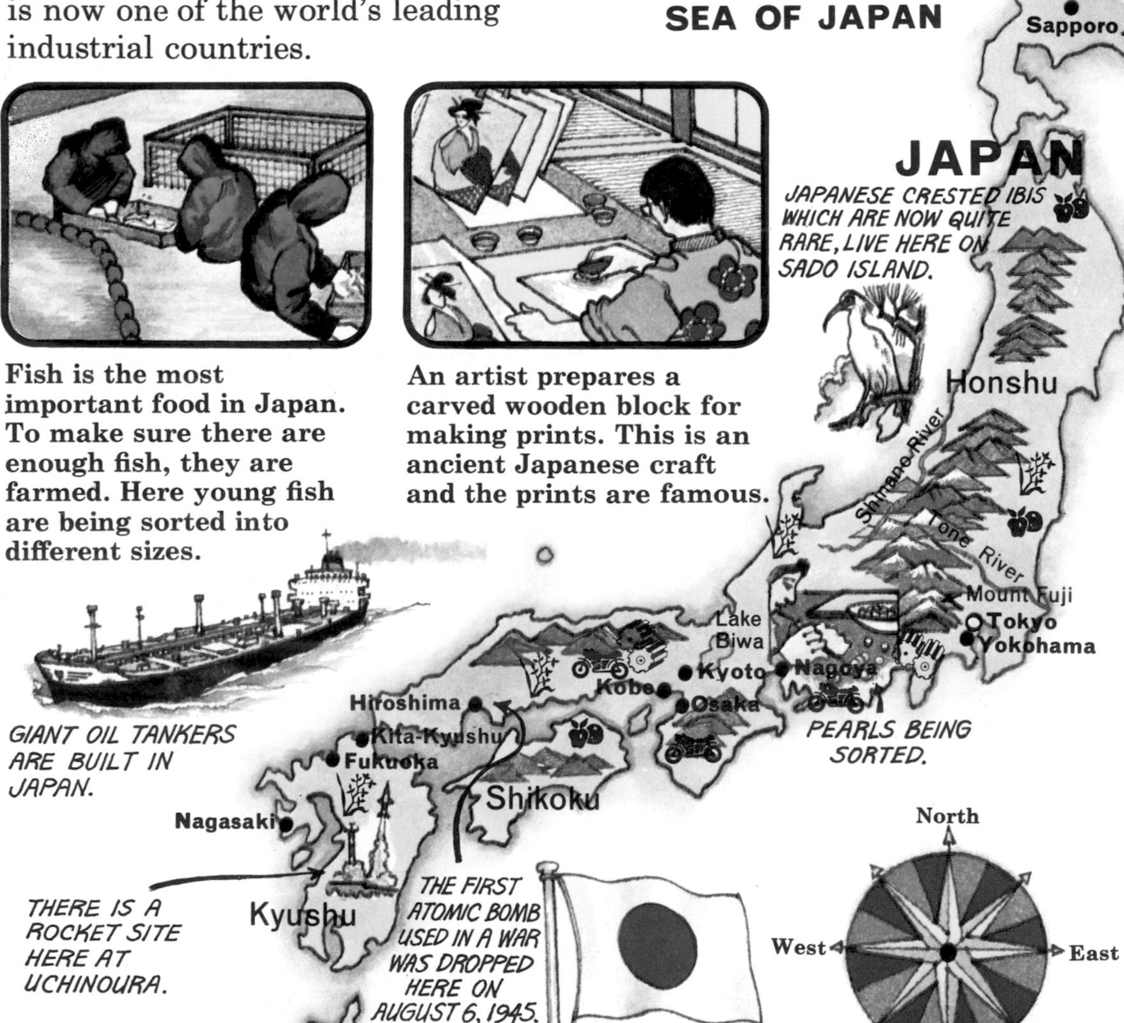

SKI-JUMPING IS POPULAR IN THE MOUNTAIN REGIONS OF JAPAN.
Hokkaido
Sapporo
SEA OF JAPAN
PACIFIC OCEAN
JAPAN
JAPANESE CRESTED IBIS WHICH ARE NOW QUITE RARE, LIVE HERE ON SADO ISLAND.
Honshu
Shinano River
Tone River
Mount Fuji
Tokyo
Yokohama
Lake Biwa
Kyoto
Nagoya
Kobe
Osaka
PEARLS BEING SORTED.
Hiroshima
Kita-Kyushu
Fukuoka
Shikoku
Nagasaki
Kyushu
GIANT OIL TANKERS ARE BUILT IN JAPAN.
THERE IS A ROCKET SITE HERE AT UCHINOURA.
THE FIRST ATOMIC BOMB USED IN A WAR WAS DROPPED HERE ON AUGUST 6, 1945.
North
West
East
South

Fish is the most important food in Japan. To make sure there are enough fish, they are farmed. Here young fish are being sorted into different sizes.

An artist prepares a carved wooden block for making prints. This is an ancient Japanese craft and the prints are famous.

Flag of Japan

The Japanese car industry is nearly the largest in the world. Japanese cars are small and cheap to run.

Japan builds more ships than any other country in the world. It has over 1,000 shipyards.

The Poles

It is so cold at the Poles that they are covered with ice all year round. At the South Pole the ice covers a huge piece of land called Antarctica. Scientists go there to study the land, but no one lives there. The coldest place on Earth is in Antarctica.

At the North Pole there is no land at all, just a vast sheet of ice floating on the sea. The area round the North Pole is called the Arctic. In winter, most of the sea freezes over. Then, the land inside the Arctic Circle is joined up by ice.

People called Eskimos live in the Arctic. They travel across the ice hunting seals and caribou, which are a type of reindeer. When the Eskimos are out hunting they build shelters called igloos out of bricks of ice.

Greenland belongs to the country of Denmark. About 51,000 people live there.

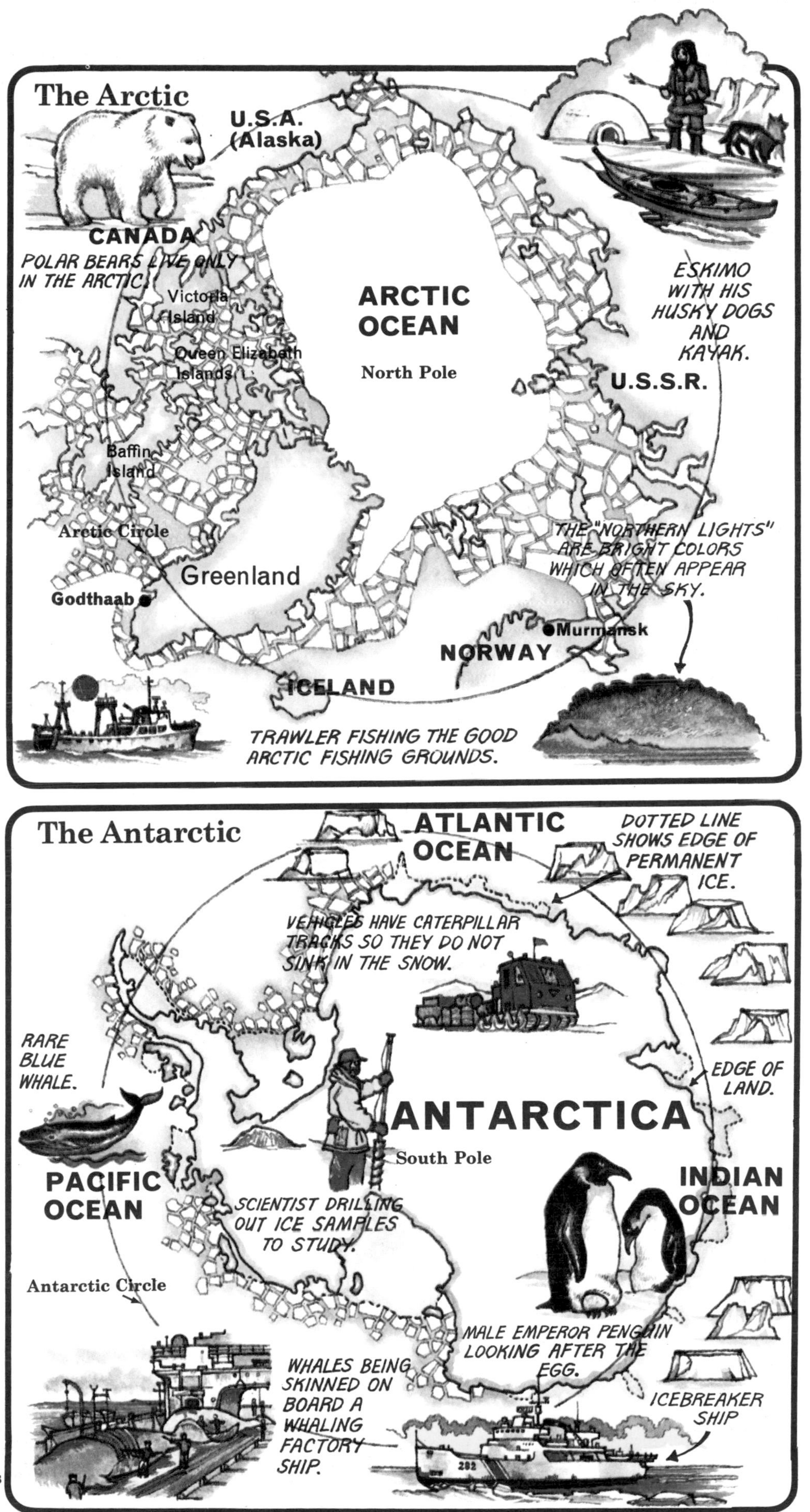

The Arctic
U.S.A. (Alaska)
CANADA
POLAR BEARS LIVE ONLY IN THE ARCTIC.
Victoria Island
Queen Elizabeth Islands
ARCTIC OCEAN
North Pole
ESKIMO WITH HIS HUSKY DOGS AND KAYAK.
U.S.S.R.
Baffin Island
Arctic Circle
Greenland
Godthaab
THE "NORTHERN LIGHTS" ARE BRIGHT COLORS WHICH OFTEN APPEAR IN THE SKY.
Murmansk
NORWAY
ICELAND
TRAWLER FISHING THE GOOD ARCTIC FISHING GROUNDS.
The Antarctic
ATLANTIC OCEAN
DOTTED LINE SHOWS EDGE OF PERMANENT ICE.
VEHICLES HAVE CATERPILLAR TRACKS SO THEY DO NOT SINK IN THE SNOW.
RARE BLUE WHALE.
EDGE OF LAND.
ANTARCTICA
South Pole
PACIFIC OCEAN
INDIAN OCEAN
SCIENTIST DRILLING OUT ICE SAMPLES TO STUDY.
Antarctic Circle
MALE EMPEROR PENGUIN LOOKING AFTER THE EGG.
WHALES BEING SKINNED ON BOARD A WHALING FACTORY SHIP.
ICEBREAKER SHIP

The maps on this page are different from the rest of the maps in this book. They are drawn as if you were looking at the Earth from above and below.

Scale

0 400 800 1200 1600 2000 2400 2800 Km

0 200 400 600 800 1000 1200 1400 1600 Miles

Australia

Australia is as big as the United States of America, but only about 18 million people live there. Most people live on the east coast where the land is good for farming. Inland there is hot, dry desert where hardly anyone lives.

The north is very hot and wet all year round. Sometimes there are dangerous 200 k.p.h. winds called typhoons.

New Zealand is about 1,900 km from Australia. We have shown it closer so that it fits on the page. Over 3 million people live there.

European explorers found these countries about 300 years ago. The only people living there then were the Aborigines in Australia and the Maoris in New Zealand. Since then many Europeans have settled there too.

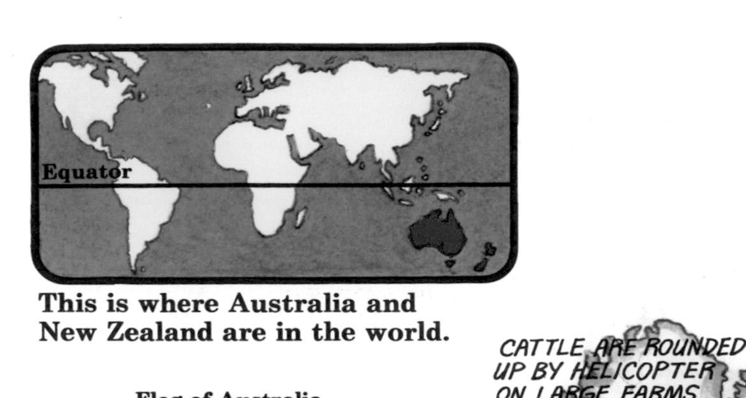
Equator

This is where Australia and New Zealand are in the world.

Flag of Australia
Darwin
CATTLE ARE ROUNDED UP BY HELICOPTER ON LARGE FARMS.
Wyndham
Broome
NORTHERN TERRITORY
IRON ORE IS MINED IN THIS AREA
Great Sandy Desert
LAKES IN THE DESERT DRY UP WHEN THERE IS NO RAIN.
Lake Disappointment
ABORIGINE PAINTING ON BARK
River Gascoyne
Gibson Desert
WESTERN AUSTRALIA
AYERS ROCK—BIGGEST ROCK IN THE WORLD.
CRAYFISH ARE CAUGHT HERE.
SHARKS
AUSTRALIA
Great Victoria Desert
Geraldton
INDIAN OCEAN
SHIPS ARE BUILT AT THE PORT OF WHYALLA.
A GOLD NUGGET. THE RICHEST GOLDFIELDS ARE AT KALGOORLIE.
Kalgoorlie
Perth
North
West
East
South
EUCALYPTUS, OR GUM, TREES GROW IN AUSTRALIA. THEIR VERY HARD WOOD IS USEFUL.
Albany

Grape vines were brought to Australia from Europe. Half the grapes are dried to make raisins and sultanas. The rest are made into wine.

Peaches, pears, apricots, pineapples and many other fruits grow in Australia and New Zealand. A lot of the fruit is put into cans.

About a third of the world's wool comes from Australia. Sheep shearers cut the wool from the sheep very quickly.

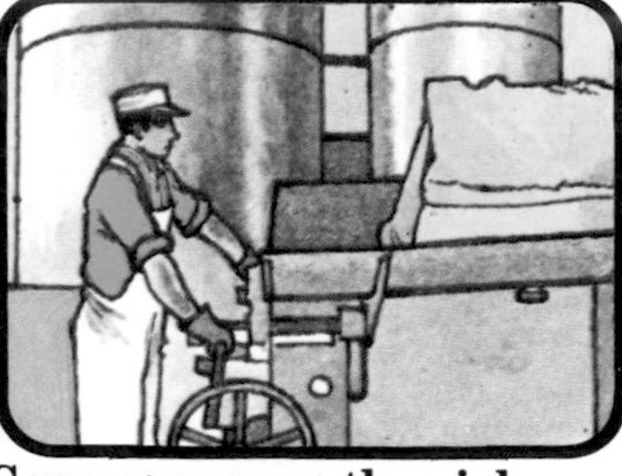

Cows graze on the rich grasslands of New Zealand. Some of their milk is made into butter and cheese in dairy factories like this.

Wheat is grown in these countries. Scientists have grown special kinds which can be planted in the very dry places.

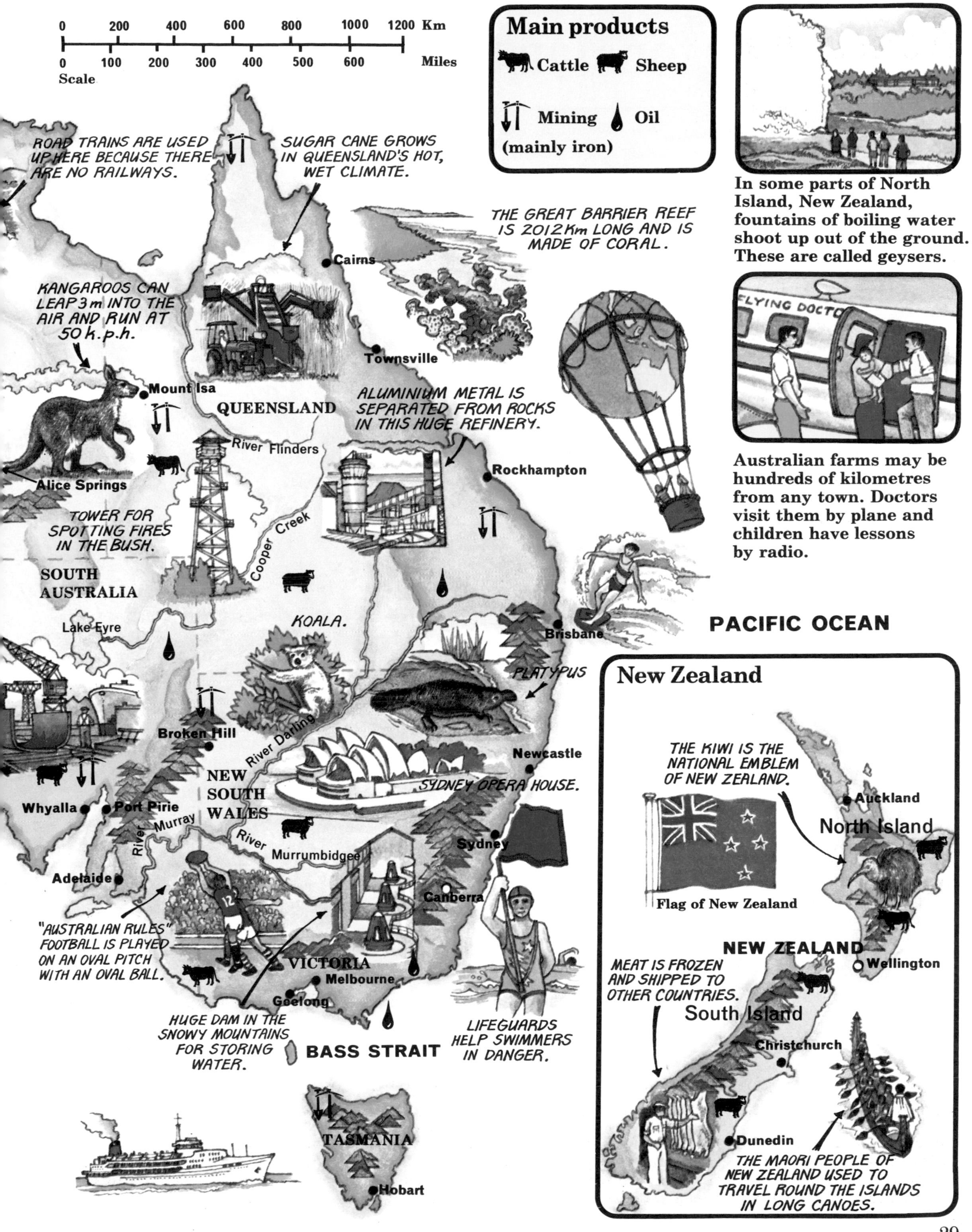
0 200 400 600 800 1000 1200 Km
0 100 200 300 400 500 600 Miles
Scale
Main products
Cattle
Sheep
Mining (mainly iron)
Oil
In some parts of North Island, New Zealand, fountains of boiling water shoot up out of the ground. These are called geysers.
FLYING DOCTO
Australian farms may be hundreds of kilometres from any town. Doctors visit them by plane and children have lessons by radio.
ROAD TRAINS ARE USED UP HERE BECAUSE THERE ARE NO RAILWAYS.
SUGAR CANE GROWS IN QUEENSLAND'S HOT, WET CLIMATE.
THE GREAT BARRIER REEF IS 2012Km LONG AND IS MADE OF CORAL.
Cairns
KANGAROOS CAN LEAP 3m INTO THE AIR AND RUN AT 50k.p.h.
Townsville
Mount Isa
QUEENSLAND
ALUMINIUM METAL IS SEPARATED FROM ROCKS IN THIS HUGE REFINERY.
River Flinders
Rockhampton
Alice Springs
TOWER FOR SPOTTING FIRES IN THE BUSH.
Cooper Creek
SOUTH AUSTRALIA
PACIFIC OCEAN
Lake Eyre
KOALA.
Brisbane
PLATYPUS
Broken Hill
River Darling
Newcastle
NEW SOUTH WALES
SYDNEY OPERA HOUSE.
Whyalla
Port Pirie
River Murray
River Murrumbidgee
Sydney
Adelaide
Canberra
"AUSTRALIAN RULES" FOOTBALL IS PLAYED ON AN OVAL PITCH WITH AN OVAL BALL.
VICTORIA
Melbourne
Geelong
HUGE DAM IN THE SNOWY MOUNTAINS FOR STORING WATER.
BASS STRAIT
LIFEGUARDS HELP SWIMMERS IN DANGER.
TASMANIA
Hobart
New Zealand
THE KIWI IS THE NATIONAL EMBLEM OF NEW ZEALAND.
Flag of New Zealand
Auckland
North Island
NEW ZEALAND
Wellington
MEAT IS FROZEN AND SHIPPED TO OTHER COUNTRIES.
South Island
Christchurch
Dunedin
THE MAORI PEOPLE OF NEW ZEALAND USED TO TRAVEL ROUND THE ISLANDS IN LONG CANOES.

Colour Key for Maps

Grasslands and prairies —usually quite flat areas.

Deserts—very dry areas where hardly anything grows.

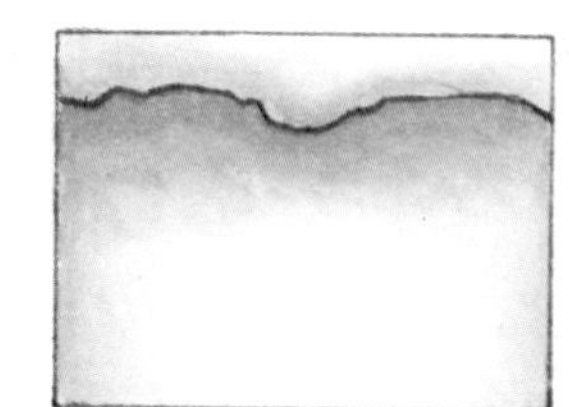

Tundra—cold treeless areas where ice melts for a short time each year.

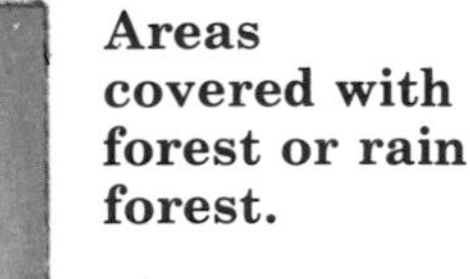

Areas covered with forest or rain forest.

High, mountainous areas. Peaks with white on them are snow-capped.

Pack ice—areas of partly frozen sea. Some of it melts in summer.

Sea coast.

Border with a country which appears on another map.

Solid ice. These areas are covered with thick ice all year.

Index of Place Names

Names in CAPITAL LETTERS are countries. Names in **bold type** are capital cities.

General Index